"Between These Thighs"

"Between These Thighs"

Erotic Short Stories & Poetry

FOR HIM

Book One of The Cindarotica Collection

Written By: Cinda "Cin" Cianelli

authorHOUSE®

AuthorHouse™
1663 Liberty Drive
Bloomington, IN 47403
www.authorhouse.com
Phone: 1-800-839-8640

Published by AuthorHouse   03/01/2012

ISBN: 978-1-4685-4991-1 (sc)
ISBN: 978-1-4685-4990-4 (hc)
ISBN: 978-1-4685-4989-8 (e)

Library of Congress Control Number: 2012902099

Special thanks to my World-Renowned Front-Cover Photographer, Richard A Urycki, of Captured Visions Photography, in Las Vegas, Nevada USA; +1.702.468.4586 www.CapturedVisionsPhotography.com.

Specializing in: Fashion, Model Portfolio, Nature, Landscape, Hotel/Resort, Restaurant, Mune items, Personal Collections, Virtual Tours, Commissions... Very little Photoshop, if any, is ever applied to my work. My passion of imaging always directs me to the end result.

My thanks to Brian DeCania of Las Vegas, Nevada for taking time to do a quick photo shoot and contribute to five images of me, for the inside cover of my book.

DEDICATIONS

I dedicate this book to all of the men out there in this world that made me feel something through conversations, meeting, writing, and video chatting. Without all of you, there would be no book.

Thank you. (Smile)

TABLE OF CONTENTS

FOREWORD

My friend, Cinda "Cin" Cianelli has a unique style of writing that evokes feelings in the reader like no other writer can do.

Her style is soft and gentle and yet powerful and provocative. It stirs the emotions by painting vivid pictures that leave you breathless and wanting more.

Each story captures the essence of erotica and takes you to a place within yourself that you did not even know existed.

This book is one of those books you cannot put down once you start reading it. It stimulates the imagination and arouses the emotions to a new level. It explores erotica by arousing the emotions using a unique combination of imagery and words.

Cin has an ability to take a sexual experience and make it something everyone can identify with and experience mentally as they read.

Each story addresses a particular aspect of erotica and the related sexual experiences. The words come to life as you read them, transporting you to the experience itself and ecstasy that ensues.

If you have never read a book about erotica, this is the perfect book to start with and I guarantee you will enjoy every exhilarating story, and upcoming books from her collection.

Cin is a good friend of mine, and a very fine Writer. She is talented, funny, intelligent, and a Sexy Ebony Queen—Erotica is truly her baby.

I read one of her stories once—and then I woke up!

Finding myself chained to a sink leaking. Hahahaha!!!

Yeah, that is exactly what I said and thought when she said that she was, one day, going to collar me, and leave me chained naked to the kitchen sink.

"What??!!"

I do not know what was exactly going through her head, but being collared, naked, and chained to the kitchen sink is just not inviting to me, but Cin, we can still be friends though!!

Hahahahaha.

Again, I'm sure that everyone who picks up a copy of this book will enjoy each and every story, and she is going to kill you all with the audio book; her voice is really that sensual.

I'm honored to be this very talented woman's friend. Oh, and none of the stories are about me mind you. (lol)

Wishing my intelligent, clever, erotic, sugar britches, cottontail storyteller the best blessings and much success! She always gets on me about calling her "Sugar Britches" and "Cottontail", but I do it anyway, because I can. Hahahahaha.

Smooches to you Cin,

From DC, With Love!

Comedian Kevin Anthony

HBO Def Comedy Jam All-Star, BET Comic View, Showtime at the Apollo, Comedian Kevin Anthony: Can be found website: www. Kevanthony.com Intro . . . Facebook

PREFACE

In being asked if a woman's orgasm is the same as a man's? My immediate reply was, "I do not know." (Giggles)

This question plagued me for some time, causing me to go deep into thought for the answer.

How could it be? How could any person's orgasm be the same or exactly the same? Think about it. How could a person even know exactly how another person feel, let alone, their orgasms?

We can tell each other how we feel or felt, and describe it in great detail to one another, but can the person that is listening grasp it to where they can truly say that they felt the same exact feelings? No. (Smile)

I am sure that many papers, articles, columns and books have been written on this subject, and I must admit that I have not read any of them. Mainly to not sway from what I am feeling and feel when I see my words come alive onto paper, or to feel what I feel, when I am wrapped in his arms, melting into him.

I try to keep my mind clear of the chatter, and of words that really have nothing to do with what I feel at that moment, while in that moment of ecstasy. This, I believe, is what makes my orgasms more than frequent, more than multiple, more than the norm, actually beyond what you could ever imagine.

I want to express to you, through my stories how you men, make us women feel by using my words to stir up your passion deep within you; allowing you to know how we, or I, myself, experience the moment from the beginning to the end.

I am a very visual, extremely sensual, and sexual female that feels everything, and just from a word, a sentence, a feeling, a man's thick wrists, his low and/or deep voice, or the shape of a man's eyes will start me to see visions that come alive right before my eyes, manifesting itself into stories.

I really hope that you enjoy my stories and also hope that you will be anxious to purchase the second book from The Cindarotica Collection—"I Am Cin!!" The stories are more intense (see the teaser in the back section of this book), more photos will be added, and each book, as well as this one, will also be available in audio-book format for those that do not like to read, have time to read, or would like to hear the steamy seduction of my voice read the book to you. (Smile)

However, I must warn you now, that the audio book is severely and intensely sexual. (Cinful Smile)

Enjoy and thank you . . .

ACKNOWLEDGEMENTS

A truly heart-felt thanks goes out to Actor, Singer, and Friend: Frederick B. Owens, for putting me more in touch with my erotic side, and giving me the courage to overcome my fear of it all.

Allowing me to let it shine through into my everyday life, with just his words to me in lengthy-phone conversations. And also explaining to me that I have a "Sex Voice", what it is, how to recognize it, hone in on it, and to grow comfortable with using it. Thank you for everything Fred. (Smile)

A most sincere and loving thanks to Rusty Postlewait, Professional Golfer, Friend, and Muse, whose amazingly Caribbean-Blue Eyes, rustic-sensual voice, and laid-back demeanor inspired many of the stories in this book. May we always be friends Rusty. (Smile)

Thank you to Kevin Anthony Comedian, a personal friend, for all of the funny phone conversations that kept me a bit distracted from the growing pains of my success. With all of your jokes and funny stories, you kept me laughing through it all. (Giggles) Keep them laughing handsome. (Smile)

Thank you to my good Friend, Fire Fighter, Frank Hido, from my hometown: Cleveland, Ohio. Thank you for being there for me in the beginning of all of this, and keeping in contact with me through all of my wild adventures all over America. Thank you for being the angel that watched over and protected me while I was in traveling mode. Be safe out there . . . (smile)

A special and heart felt thanks to a Beautiful Queen in her own right—Ms. Renada Carr. She is the owner of the new "Mia Bella Sorelle Salon", meaning "My Beautiful Sisters, in Italian; located in Southern Oklahoma. Where she created some of the new Cindarotica Images for my book(s), upcoming calendar, website and more.

Ms. Renada takes pampering her clients to a whole other level in public and private settings, using the most updated techniques, and products on all of her clients. Her Website information is: www. MiaBellaSorelle@yola.com and www.Tagged.com/Miabellasorelle

Thank you to Timmy Green, a newfound friend that I met in Las Vegas, shortly before returning to Europe late 2011. I want to thank you for igniting me into a blazing fire of loving feelings, and inspiring some of the stories in my second book called: "I Am Cin", as well as my up and coming dating book.

No guy has ever made me feel as girly, giggly, smiley, sexually charged, loss of breath, off-balance, intense surges of electricity through my very being, and submissive, all at the same time. (Blush) May we be in each other's lives forever—I miss you; see you soon. (Blushing)

Thank you to Hannah Marishahl, the Host of "The Seldom Seen Poets", held at 7 p.m., every Wednesday at the, Sunrise Coffee Company, located at 3130 E. Sunset Rd.; Las Vegas, Nevada.

When I first read my work in public, it was her, and her spot that allowed me to speak my words freely, taking as much time as I needed (depending on how many readers were present).

Neither her nor the other poets, writers, staff, and people that came out to hear us knew how afraid I really was; I was terrified.

No, Hannah, I had never read my work in public before, and I sincerely thank you for allowing me the opportunity to overcome my fear and shyness; to grow stronger reading my work at your venue. Whenever I am in town, I would love to feature at your spot. (Smile)

Thank you to DJ Miss Joy, and Jeffrey Bennington Grindley, Hosts of The Human Experience; located at the corner of 6th & Fremont Street Downtown Las Vegas, Nevada; at the Fremont Street Experience, inside of the Emergency Arts Building every Monday night starting at 7 p.m.

It was with you that I experienced my first club scene, and reading my work on a microphone. (Giggles) Yes, scared me stiff, but I was well received, and have been ever since. Thank you so much. (Smile)

Much, much, much love to **_The Poets' Corner_**; my favorite out of all of the open-mic venues!!!

"They are the longest running open mic venue in the City of Las Vegas, Nevada".

Mr. Ellis Rice, Ms. Pendelita Toney, and the current Host, Keith A. Brantley, founded the Poets' Corner in 1997.

They are located inside of the West Las Vegas Cultural Arts Center, at 947 West Lake Mead Blvd., Las Vegas Nevada; every third Friday of every month from 7 p.m. until they put us out!! (Giggles)

Their mission is to give voice to every poet who wants to be heard, furthermore, The Poets' Corner has been the launch pad for some of Las Vegas' most noteworthy poets such as: **Ms. China, LaBlaque, Trinity Smith, Bliss, Etch, the Host himself, Keith Brantley**, and countless others. I am more than honored to have shared an open mic, and stage performance(s) with them.

Out of all of the places to perform, I really loved reading my work at this venue the most, and truly lived for that third Friday out of every month. Keith allows you total freedom with your words, and trust me, there are not many places out there like this one, plus they offer snacks, and beverages at no cost to all that attend. (Smiles) Much love to you Keith, and may The Poets' Corner live on into future generations. (Smile) Thank you from my heart.

To Wes, Owner of The Arts Factory. Thank you for allowing me to grace your stage and microphone so many times, usually every Saturday night, and First Friday. If you have never been to this venue, it is a must! Located at the corner of Charleston & Main Street in the Arts District, downtown Las Vegas, Nevada.

Thank you, to ALL of Las Vegas' Art and Poetry Community for allowing me to speak my words freely and accepting me as an artist. As well as a big thanks to the poets, writers, dancers, musicians, bands, singers, painters, and more that I have shared the stage or events with. (Smile)

And lastly, to Claudia D'Angelo, the Host of Poetry Slam, held at the Lettere Caffé, located at San Francesco a Ripa 100 & 101; (Trastevere) Roma, Italy.

This Beautiful Italian Comedian and Poet welcomes poets from all walks of life to read there work in a competitive, but fun-for-all platform, every Monday night at 10 p.m. until the last poet standing; in which the last poet standing, wins a bottle of wine. (Smile)

This is the crowd in which I received my first standing ovation ever; the piece I read is the second story in this book called, "He Wooed Me".

Thank you Claudia, for allowing me to speak my words in English, and thank you to all who attended during my readings, that embraced my words and me. Grazie Mille Bellissima, I wish you much success in life . . . (Smile)

Again, thank you all for giving me the support and opportunity to read my words from my first book of erotica.

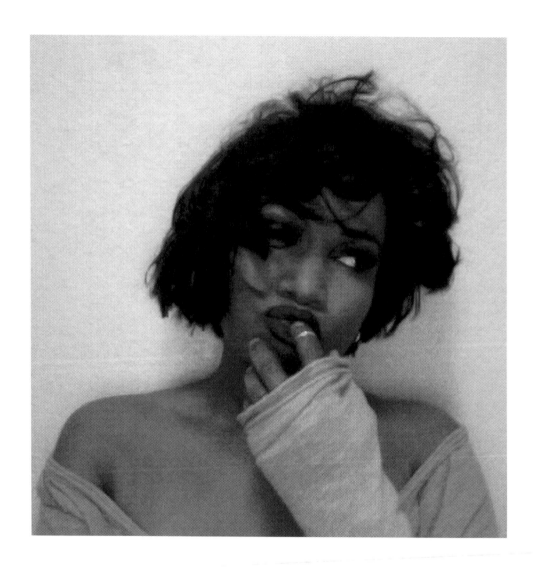

TASTE

He . . .

He told me to taste it
"Taste what?" I said.

"Taste you, to taste what you taste like,
like I taste you in the dark of night."

I taste and what I taste is the taste of love,
the taste of me,
the taste of the essence of my womanhood,
my sexuality.

My taste that he tastes, when he tastes me.

He's got me open,
open to see, open to feel the feel of me,
my being,
my soul,
and to set it all free.

Mmmmm . . .

I am feeling what he feels,
what he sees,
what he needs,
what he feels when he feels me.

Damn he's good at brining out what he brings out in me,
bringing out that "Ooooo Weeee" in me,
that passion,
that storm,
that thunder,
that arousal in me.

"Tease me." He said,
"Tease how?"

"Tease with touch,
with moves to move that body so sensually,
to make me make you want me,
to make me want me too."

"To move your body slow,
and I touch myself as it grows.

To grind, twist, and to turn;
to make slow sexual churns."

Mmmmm . . .
He aroused me . . .

Waiting . . .
Waiting for me to let him taste me.

To taste me like he tastes me when I taste myself, and I let him.

I let him let me, when we touch each other so sexually.

Mmmmm . . . don't stop baby . . .

Taste, that taste that you taste, when you taste, as I taste me.

Ooooo . . . He!!!

HE WOOED ME

He wooed me with his words . . . had me glowing, dreaming dreams, feeling feelings of aliveness beyond anything that I had ever known.

His words, softly kissing my cheek, my eyes, my lips my very breath that breathed deep in shivers of what was him.

I think now of how soft he was at capturing my attention . . . me . . . my complete focus with his damned words that caused me to drown so deep within him . . . within myself, for a moment, feeling free . . . feeling . . . lost.

His voice deep and low, with a vibration that caused my heart to beat faster, then hold still the beat!! Causing me to gasp, as I reach my hands to my chest, lowering my head, to catch my breath . . . as if it would run away . . . if I had not.

He wooed me like no other . . . speaking his magic words that collapsed my heart into his hands, feeling the roughness of his palms, the edges of his fingertips and jagged fingernails that clung to it . . . holding it . . . with his full attention . . . and with mine.

He is the distraction from my life . . . from my goals . . . from all that I am and aspire to be. Gently blowing his warm breath into me, breathing me in, not wanting to exhale me, as I am captured in this rapture of lustful silence, listening to his breathing as it nurtures my desire for him . . . intensifies my desire for him.

My gown slowly falls to the floor, catching the softness of the summer air that blew gently into the windows of my room . . . hardening my nipples . . . shivering my body . . . gasping in almost a lusty sound of silence.

I wrap my arms around me. Shielding myself from him. Not wanting to let him back into my heart, into my life, as he drops softly to his knees and slowly; he—crawls to me.

He woos me in silence, with his eyes, and his eyes showing me his thoughts that are hidden behind them, lowering them with a passion that burned through the blue of them like a silent but raging fire in the dead of night.

The love that we had made in the past, the love that he made to me, and I to him clouded my mind with silken threads of soft moaning, twisted into each other, into our arms, legs hands, fingertips and lips, softly he was and is my distraction.

Crawling to me now. In sadness and sorrow until he reaches my nakedness, looking up into my eyes as his desires burned deep inside of him. He stands before me on his knees for a moment, then rests his head into the warmness of my womb, and I feel my body tremble and jerk, as if it to scream out—"Take . . . Me . . . Now!!"

He woos me with his hands, as they lightly touch the backs of my calves, gliding up the back of my legs to rest just underneath my round firm ass. Tucking them between my thighs I . . . I feel his fingertips touch my pussy and I quiver into almost losing my balance—I am dizzy with him!!

He knows where to touch me, how to touch me, ways to touch me to make me forget that I was angry and never wanting to see his face again.

But—But I, I unravel my arms from my body to him, to touch his head, to run my fingers through his hair; pulling him closer into my womb and I feel my eyes tear up with strong emotion.

I feel his mouth kiss me on the soft patch of hair that tickled his lips; making them part while the warmth of his breath engulfed me. Releasing me. Shivering me. Teasing me, to release my raging passion I had stored within myself for him.

With my head back, and face to the ceiling, my tears roll down my face, into his hair, as I feel his tears on my belly while he grabbed and held me hard around my waist—to him.

I think of his wooing words that drowned me so deep, in the beginning, when we first met, while his soft lips kiss my navel and he look up into my eyes and my tears drip down onto his tears that soaked into his face.

"You Make Me So Weak For You Baby!!" He said, smoothly, smothering me in that low, deep and rustic voice; charming me, hypnotizing me to let him back into me; into my heart, into my soft wetness that he so desires of me.

I—I try to hold strong

But feel my body collapse around him!

Curling around him!

Withering into a puddle around him!

Of weakened desire around him!

On the floor around him!

Spreading my legs around him!

Right before him!
With Him!

I Am . . .

Free again!

Feeling . . .

Lost!

LISTEN

Listen . . .

Shhhhhhhhh . . .

Listen . . .

Aaaaaaahhhhhhh . . .

Listen deep into my words
as if you are sliding inside of me for the very first time,

And feel me.

Feel the thumping of my heart,
my blood that courses through my veins.

All of what you are feeling inside of me;
is exactly what I feel for you . . .

I have completely lost control,
allowing myself to feel you underneath my skin.

Allowing you to feel me up with your lust for me . . .
Giving myself to you in ways that makes me weaker for you.

Weak for your eyes to look into mine,
weak to see the warming of your skin;
the nervousness of your gaze,
and you,
trying to fight your urge to taste me.

Shhhhhh . . .

Listen . . .
Listen to my words
as if you can feel them echo from my pussy to your lips,
with soft juicy kisses,
sealing them to say nothing,
but to say everything.

I can see all of your dirty little secrets,
your desires;
the fire,
the lust,
and you . . .
wanting to lick me.

I can feel you.
I can feel you just the way you want me to feel you.

Listen . . .

Listen closely to how our bodies call out to each other,
wanting so badly for what we are trying to hold back.

Fighting, and wrestling with trying to walk away,
but knowing that we cannot.

So listen to me . . .

I want you,
I want to feel you inside of me.

Wetting Me . . .

Licking Me . . .

Tickling Me . . .

Sucking Me . . .

Creaming Me . . .

Touching Me . . .

Kissing Me . . .

Craving Me . . .

Deep inside of me . . .

The way you need it . . .

Make me feed it . . .

All of your desires . . .

To taste me . . .

Shhhhhhhhhhhhh . . .

LISTEN . . .

MY BIRTDAY CARD TO HIM

My perfume fills your nostrils and catch you off guard, causing you to slowly turn yourself towards the doorway of your bedroom; towards me standing there in the shadows, looking upon your chiseled body of granite; staring at those big arms, hands, abs, ass and thighs.

Waiting for everything you are going to give to me tonight baby! Just looking at you and your body gives me orgasms . . . Shittttt!!!!

"Happy Birthday Baby", I say, while leaning against the door post, dressed in a long sheer black robe; underneath it, a black heavily laced corset, six-inch heels, and seamed thigh-high stockings.

As I turn towards you, your mouth opens slowly, your eyes widen, and your breathing increases; as your nipples harden and your muscles begin to twitch; you touch and adjust yourself.

Aaaaah yessss . . . I can see your erection baby, Mmmmm . . . Hmmmm . . .

In my hands, I hold a warm tiny birthday cake, just for you; overflowing with vanilla icing that drips down over both my hands and fingers, with one lit candle placed neatly in its center. The candle flickers, casting a wicked shadow and light dance across my face and breasts.

Aaaaah . . . I sigh, walking toward you slowly, making sure that you are taking me all in. I see your body intensely jerk with excitement and your shaft rises even more.

Mmmmm . . . I say with a devilish grin on my face, "It is your birthday baby!" Smiling that smile that lets you know that I want it all tonight.

I stop and stand in front of you, extending the cake outward for you to blow out your candle, I slowly bend over to assist you, as the light from the candle dances wickedly between us. I make sure that you see my bulging breasts heaving over the top of my tightly laced corset that I wore just for you.

With that visual, you lose your breath, and I part my red full lips to assist you; your body jerks and trembles almost uncontrollably, as I softly blow the candle out for you.

When the smoke from the candle clears, you take the cake from my hands; I stare into your eyes and slowly begin to suck the icing from the tip of my finger, staring into your face, watching you . . . feeling you . . . feeling me, and all that I am going to let you take from me tonight baby.

Reaching out to your face, I smear my icing covered fingers across your lips, parting them to slowly insert them into your mouth with no resistance from you, and you lick your tongue in between them; sucking, slowly, licking; moaning with every movement of them.

"That's nice baby, I like that—I like it all" you moan with a mischievous smile to your face.

I smear some of the icing onto your chin, neck, nipples, and then to the top of my breasts, as you moan that low deep growling sound of pleasure that only you know how to arouse me with. I then smear the icing onto my lips and neck; then slowly drop the sheer robe to the floor, revealing it all—everything!!

THIS IS YOUR BIRTHDAY CARD FROM ME BABY!!

Yessss . . .

You watch my robe fall slowly to the floor; your body shakes, as your eyes trail up my long and shapely legs, enjoying every part of me. You gaze slowly up my body to see my three fingers stuffed deep into my mouth, sucking intensely; licking the last of the icing from my fingers. I reach down to you and hold your chin in my hand, looking down into your eyes,

"It is your birthday baby." I say in a low and sensual tone, softly smiling.

Your eyes open wide, then lower almost instantly, intensely, animalistically, as you move to stand and touch my breasts that are pulsating with intense breathing and anticipation.

I aggressively push you backwards onto the bed, reach down and slowly pull my panties to the side, smear the vanilla icing from your tiny birthday cake onto my pussy. "Mmmmm, that feels soooo gooood", I moan with pleasure.

You sit up pulling yourself to the edge of the bed, licking your lips, eagerly waiting my next move. I stand in front of you with my legs parted, and direct you to slowly pull my sheer g-string panties down around my ankles; your hands tremble uncontrollably and your shaft jerks with a raging force, while you rub your hands up and down my seamed stockings, sneaking glances into my face.

"Aaaaah yessss baby, I like this birthday present", you whisper in a deep growl, raising up from me stepping out of my panties, parting my legs wider, positioning myself for what I know you want to give to me tonight.

Your face meets my icing-covered pussy, and I can feel the hotness of your breath on it. You pause staring in excitement, while it swells and opens like a flower to you, seeping its juices.

You look upward into my eyes, as I stand over you, smiling and trembling for you to taste me. "Have a taste." I say, looking down at you; guiding your head into me with my hand.

You dive into my vanilla icing, sending jolts through my body as you lick it frantically from my juiciness. I jerk and grind into your mouth, with uncontrollable orgasms; knees buckling, back arching, strong convulsions of pleasure bolting through me—through the both of us. "Damn baby you are so good", I cry out sinking into the twirling softness of your tongue.

I grab the back of your head and press your face deeper into my swollen pussy, grinding to the rhythm of your tongue. "Ooooo baby", I scream out while you continue to suck away the last of the vanilla, then come up for air, licking your lips, looking into my eyes with a hunger that sent another orgasm through the core of my soul.

Mmmmm . . . "Happy Birthday Baby", I giggle loudly, and you quickly fling me over onto the bed causing my ass to be mounted up and into the air.

"I am not finished with you yet baby", you say in a deep growl. I lie there shaking and quaking with orgasms, then turn to look back; I see you drop to your knees and bury your face deep into my thick swollen wetness, and with both your big strong hands you begin to caress, grip, and spank the thickness of my round ass; then lick and kiss it.

I scream out with intense pleasure, as my body shoots off of your mouth like a rocket across the bed, barely able to catch my breath from cumming so hard.

I turn onto my back, and dig my heels deep into your bed, propping myself up on your pillows, positioning myself in the center of your California King size playground. Waiting, waiting for what is next, for what you want to give to me; Mmmmm, for what you want to make me feel.

Still with my high-heeled shoes, thigh-high stockings, and corset on, I begin to prepare myself for what was coming next; after all it is your birthday, and I am yours, yours for the taking. However you want it. However you want me.

I watch as you stand there, slowly unbuttoning your button-fly jeans, staring at me intensely, as I stare at the huge bulge pushing out against your pants.

Your shaft is so hard and stiff that it gets caught just underneath the band of your boxer briefs. You reach down to free it and it pops out thick, long, hard, and ready to enter me. Thumping, throbbing, pulsing like an angry beast.

"Damn baby, this is going to be soooo damn gooood", you say, staring into my face.

I grasp the thick comforter with both hands as you crawl onto the bed towards me, I gasp, as my body began to tremble, quivering, quaking with eyes open wide and wild, thinking out loud about the size of it.

"How is all of that going to fit baby?" I ask with fear in my voice.

You mount yourself over me, kissing and licking the icing from my lips and breasts. "You're going to be just fine baby, I am going to make you feel so good", you speak with a smoothness to your voice.

I try to relax, but nervously lick the last of the icing from your chin, neck and nipples, thinking silently to myself, "What have I gotten myself into?"

"Are you ready for what I am going to give to you baby?" "Are you ready for me?" You say, growling and moaning, as you began to sink your thick hard shaft into my wet, tight, pussy.

"No baby, I do not think that I can handle, handdlllllleee, hh—handdlle it!!!

Ooooh Shittttt Baby . . . Wait!!!

HAPPY BIRTHDAY BABY!!!!

HE IS

Sitting here in the darkness of my room . . . thinking . . . thinking that he could have been the one, and I walked away on the verge of him—asking me to stay.

His kisses haunting me now, burning a fire deep into my wet moist place, causing me to dream, to daydream of what could have been, not realizing until now that he was . . . my Italia.

He was the whispers that called to me, that swooned my body, that made its way underneath my skin, crawling, tickling, and teasing me just how I wanted to be teased . . . how I needed . . . to be teased.

His kisses were the kiss of my king, my knight, my love that made my heart take flight. Feeling his hands grab my body, pulling me into him, tucking me into his warm embrace.

My eyes close now, almost feeling that moment again, that one night that we shared together, not wanting to let go of that new feeling that hit us both like a ton of bricks.

Walking hand in hand, arm in arm, stretching the night out as long as we could. Sneaking glances, and touching fingertips that sparked light, flaming into desire, stopping to look into each other's eyes that sparkled like stars in the moonlit sky.

And now—I sit here alone, with thoughts of his lips to mine, awakening me like the sun, warming me with hands touching my nude body as I lay myself backwards onto my bed, with a spinning head—full of him, and allowing my hands to touch myself in all the places that I would have let him touch me—if I had stayed.

I see his eyes open wide as his face levels to mine, then lower as his breath escapes him. I feel his lips trembling and warm, drowning me into a deep passion. I lose my breath, looking at him through squinting eyes, pulling back, not able to speak—weak!

Turning belly down now, while my body stirs into my covers, I grab hold of my pillow, focusing on his tallness, his thickness, his lips, his eyes, his strong thighs and the way that he looked at me from across the room.

I smell his smell and it is driving me insane; I feel the pain creep into my veins—hurting, hurting so sharply, that it feels like it could be death.

Death of the not knowing; not knowing what it would have felt like . . . to wake up wrapped in his arms.

Closing my eyes, I run my hands across my nipples, pinching them between lusting fingers, then opening them wide to the feel of it shrill through lusty parts of me. Connecting my body to jolt into recognizing the tears that race down my face into my ears, disappearing into my hair as I pull it, with a tight fist, as if it was him.

To know . . . what it would feel like, I pull it hard and harder away from my face with parted lips of ecstasy. Moaning his name, pushing my hips softly towards the ceiling, but then quickly relax to not feel the cumming of my cum.

"Wait"

Mumbling aloud as my body rest into the center of my bed, nude, with knees to the sky, legs apart, fingers stirring the firm, swollenness of my clit.

"Wait"

Breathing broken breaths of the fire that he makes me feel, desire, desires so strong, I cannot prolong it!

Slowly—I move my hips up and down, round and round, sinking fingers to my sound, moaning in steaminess, pounding heartbeat in distress, pumping, grinding, lusting, thrusting, feeling my pussy swell in my hand.

And I scream!!!

I scream for him!!!

I scream for him to come to me, for him to cum inside of me, deep inside of my warmth that surrounds my fingers now; convulsing to the sound of his name echoing loud through ringing ears, and my tears.

While I close my eyes . . .

And the image of him . . .

Slowly . . .

Disappears.

DAYDREAMING YOU

I was daydreaming about you today, and the way you would stare at me; it made me feel so warm inside.

I thought about how it would be if we made love, how I would lie there totally nude in your bed and you would slowly and softly touch every inch of my body.

I would quiver and gasp with the strong orgasms that you would cause just by touching me gently with your fingertips. Brushing across my body with soft feathery strokes, as if to be a painter, painting a romantic masterpiece.

How you would stare into my face, as if you absorbed every part and, every thought of me; then slowly lifting yourself up, lowering your face to mine, while we locked eyes, and you place the most wet, the most juicy, the most soft, sensual and deep kisses on my lips. You climb on top of me, and I could feel your hairy chest brush across my already erect nipples.

I quiver again, trembling, shaking, convulsing with stronger and stronger orgasms. Aaaaah, with your kisses getting stronger, deeper, sweeter, and more passionate. I slowly spread my legs apart and I can feel you at my door, slowly stabbing, gently parting me to enter into my soft sweet spot.

I can feel you, I can taste your lips, I can smell you; feel your breaths as you gasp trying to enter my tightness. I can feel my body tense with pain and pleasure as you whisper into my ear softly, "Relax Baby, Just Relax", while your warm lips brush across my ear.

Cinda "Cin" Cianelli

I could feel your hot breath breathing intensely on my neck.
Just that alone sent a jolt through my entire body that caused
you to enter me instantly, slipping suddenly into that warm moist
place.

"Ooooo Shit Baby", you say to me, "You are soooo fucking tight,
my God!!"

And you kiss me deeper slowly sinking, slowly inching deeper
inside of me.

Mmmmm Damn . . .

I feel your hands grab my round plump ass squeezing it, then
slide them downward to my thighs, and spread my legs open even
wider.

"Ooooh No, Baby Wait", I say frantically,

"It's to much . . .

I can't . . .

It's too big . . .

It's too Mmmmm . . .

It's too . . .

Oh Shit . . .

It's fucking . . .

Oh My God!!!!

It's Soooo . . .

Yessss . . .

Ooooh Fuck . . .

Oh Yessss, baby . . .

That 's it . . .

Like that . . .

Yes baby . . .

Oh yeah . . .

Ooooo Shittttt!!"

You pull yourself deeper into me, burying it deeper as I pant anxiously, pulling your hair, lightly scratching your back, biting your shoulders, and kissing you with the most deep and passionate kisses I have ever given to anyone . . .

Mmmmm, this is what I daydreamed about as I thought of you today baby.

I am daydreaming YOU . . .

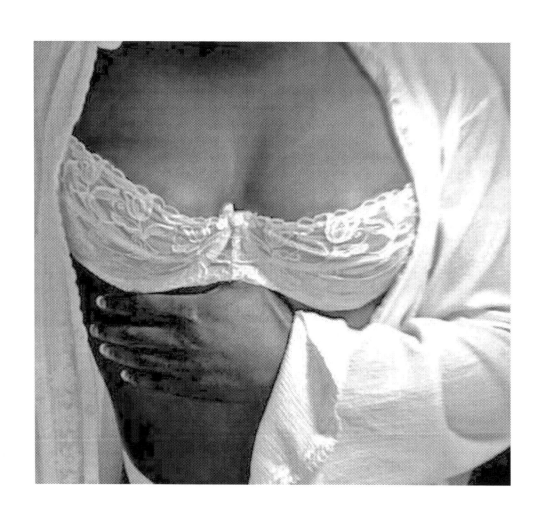

EARLY MORNING

It is early morning, and I can hear nothing but silence and your deep slow breathing.

I love being snuggled in the warmth of you, the warmth of your thick strong arms that swallow me up as if I were a child.

Feeling the hair on your arms, caressing my skin like a warm soft blanket, and feeling your heartbeat vibrate through to mine. Beating the same slow rhythm, I relax deeper—into you.

I lie there, staring into the sheer curtains as the sun rises slowly, playing its shadow and light games on the walls. Not wanting to move, not wanting to give this feeling away just yet. Wanting this moment to last forever. Dreading the time and the feel of when it must end.

Our bodies begin to shift in slow motion, and I feel the softness of your lips press gently against my back, sending a warming sensation through me that lit me up—like the sun.

I drown into you wrapping your arm around my waist, as you intertwine your leg over and into mine; then spread your large hand open on my belly, you pull me softly into your erection, and I—melt.

Aaaaah . . .

I love early morning sex with you, and the hardened stiffness of your shaft, that stands erect commanding to be touched, to be felt, to be sunken deep inside of me.

I reach back to grip it into my hand as our heartbeats quicken, and the warmth of your breath releases onto my back causing me to shiver; causing me to push my ass into you, wanting you, feeling you stiffen and grind softly and slowly into me, throbbing and pulsing in thickness.

My head spins with the feeling and the sound of only our deep breathing, and the sounds of our bodies shifting and grinding into each other, in and out of the covers on our bed.

I feel your moistness oozing into anxiousness. I want you inside of me.

Deep—inside of me.

You turn me over to my back gently, softly kissing my arms, my shoulders, then my breast. Holding it in the palm of your hand, you pinch my nipple firmly between your fingers, then take it into your mouth, pulling, sucking, and licking it . . . Mmmmm . . . Biting it.

My body quakes with rage, bouncing my breasts back and forth, as you wildly mount me breathing heavy, groaning deep causing my juices to ooze out greeting your shaft as it plunges deep inside of me.

Damn!!!

I am drowning into you, tossing my legs up into the air like I was a rag doll and you were a mad man, and I am liking the wildness of how you are handling me . . . How you are fucking me.

I look down as you enter me deep, then deeper, spreading me, gasping me into unspoken words. Silenced with widened eyes on the edge of tears from the pain, and the biting of my lower lip from the pleasure . . . of . . . it . . . all!!

Moaning, groaning, wrestling, tussling, tangled into wet covers of our juices, plunging deep; so deep that I breathe inward to scream, biting your shoulder, leaving teeth-mark kisses on your skin, scaring your flesh with my nails, into red trails of lust down your back; sinking them deep into your ass.

You ride me hard, and harder, creaming me, screaming me into wanting more, biting my nipples, talking dirty to me, as our bodies begin to drip sweat with my legs mounted up over your shoulders, and the bed begins to rock into a squealing, creaking distress.

I turn to your face, as we lock eyes; and I came so hard, while the smacking noises from my wetness and your thrusting hard into me fill the air, drowning me, drowning us.

Your words muffle from deep within your throat, raging forth your voice into moans, and shouts of intense growling as you pulled out of me and shot your juices all over my breasts, my belly, and my swollen pussy, jerking yourself into a rage of weakened lust truly spent, as I was spent, as we were spent and drowning into the dizziness of our orgasms.

You fall to my side and we both lie there, breathing heavy, with quivering bodies; sensually drained into a lusty wetness—weakened by the early morning.

IN THE RAIN

I woke up late this morning, hearing you stir around just outside of our bedroom door that leads to the patio.

Mmmmm . . . I moan, turning over slowly, remembering only snippets of last night's party; our last party of summer, and all the laughter that we shared with our friends; it brought a smile to my face. I kept smelling the smell of roses though, even in my dreams, and I did not understand why.

As the A/C kicked on and blew cold air across the back of my legs, I tucked them underneath the softness of the covers, while clutching the pillow beneath my head, not wanting to get up just yet.

I hear you slide a few chairs across the deck, you clear your throat and I lift slowly, with my hair falling over my face, blocking part of my view, and your white dress shirt that I wore to bed last night is twisted in such a way that it constricts my movement to move any further.

You are up early baby; thinking to myself, as I pull my hair away from my face in clumps, then reach for a glass of water that sat on the nightstand.

As my eyes began to focus, I see the beautiful red roses in a vase with a card next to them. I swish the water around in my mouth and unravel your shirt, as I move to sit up and swing my legs over the side of the bed. I anxiously open the card and it read, "It is going to rain today baby", signed with a smiley face.

I sit there on the side of the bed, with my thighs aching from yesterday's early morning run. I lean forward to let the blood rush to my head, as my hair dropped down almost touching the floor, stretching out my back, my arms; then my legs.

You continue to slide chairs and tables across the patio, putting the last of everything in its place. Still sitting bent over the side of the bed stretching, I look between a gap in my hair to see your body shimmering from your sweat; your shoulders and chest muscles bulging and twitching with every move that you made.

Mmmmm, I likey. (Smile)

You have on those, nearly see-through, white linen lounging pants that I bought you last week, and I see that you do not have on any underwear. You left them untied to drape down just below your waste and cling to the top part of your ass, while your shaft dangles in all of its girthiness.

Damn baby, you are so sexy. I instantly become wet just watching you move about.

You pause, while drinking a bottled water, looking over the yard, the pool, and at all of the empty bottles of liquors and beer strewn over the grass; you grab a bag and begin to pick them up.

I scurry to the bathroom, brush my teeth, wipe the smeared mascara from underneath my eyes, loosely pile my hair onto the top of my head, grab the small card that was attached to the roses, then walked over to the patio door, and tap tap tap on the glass with my fingernails.

You look at me and smile, pointing to the sky with a boyish grin on your face; you look away to move a chair that was in front of you, then you look at me again, this time with a smile—then with intensity.

You stand there as I remove some of the hair from my face, tucking it behind my ears and focus on your eyes. I bite my bottom lip in nervousness as your shaft thickens and began to rise; I blush at the site of it.

Lifting the card to my face, I cover my eyes, slowly peeking from behind it, and blushing at how fast your shaft had risen to me standing there behind the glass in nothing but your shirt.

Standing on my toes, as if to have on high-heel shoes; I cross one leg in front of the other and lean against the doorpost, smiling coyly. I motion my lips to silently say thank you for the card and roses; you smile and wink your eye to me.

Sliding the door open slowly, I could smell it, the rain; the raw fresh smell of rain. That smell always reminded me of sex. A raw, animalistic, lusty-type sex.

I stood there while the wind gently blew the smell of it into my face, and through my hair, allowing it to caress my long legs that gracefully stood there on tiptoes.

"Come here baby", your mouth and finger motioned to me. I smile as I stare into your sexy eyes, with your big shirt swallowing me up, envisioning all the things that you would do to me if I came to you.

"Baby—come here please." You say again, snapping me out of that thought with the smoothness of your voice. I walk slowly through the door, focusing on your eyes, and your bed hair—smiling.

I approach you with my hands down to my side, as the sleeves of your shirt completely cover my hands and only the very tip of the card is showing. Walking towards you slowly on tiptoes, I try not to look at your erection.

The closer I got to you, the wetter and more nervous I became; knowing that you were going to take me in the worst way.

Suddenly, right before I was arms length in front of you, the warm summer rain began to fall heavily, almost silently at first, then it came down thick, in a steady pour. We both stopped to look at it, smiling, feeling aroused, watching it as it hypnotized us to the point of breathlessness and excitement.

You turn to look at me with a mischievous look on your face and began to slowly walk backwards into the rain from underneath the covered patio, smiling temptingly.

Watching you, I felt my pussy explode with its warm juices.

Not taking your eyes off of me, the rain began to wet your strong, muscular frame—I watched and I melted.

It begins soak into your hair, causing it to lie flat, and cover your forehead, down to your thick, dark, eyebrows, while you spread your arms wide, welcoming its touch.

I watch the rain, as it wets your lounging pants and expose your shaft that was not affected at all by its coolness. The weight of your wet pants began to slide down more, exposing your pelvic area and the bulge of muscles in its creases and I shiver as my nipples harden—I like that part of you.

"It feels good baby, come here, come to me!" You speak softly with a boyish smile on your face, while your eyes dance with excitement.

I giggle and walk towards the edge of the patio, sitting the card on the table and rolling the sleeves of your shirt up past my wrists.

I step out from underneath the patio cover onto the warm grass, as the blades of it push itself up between my toes tickling my feet. My nipples harden more, sending a jolt of pleasure down to my sweet spot, taking the smile from my face and replacing it with passion, as the rain tapped my large nipples making your wet shirt expose them to you.

You stand there watching me, watching the wetness come down and make love to me, and me giving in to the feeling of it, while I watched you watching me, and the rain wetting both our bodies. Your smile slowly disappears as you begin to walk towards me, and I slowly back away with our eyes locked onto each other's.

I do not know why, but when it comes to having sex with you, you make me feel bashful, and at the same time, you make me feel intoxicated, almost drunk with lust for you. The anticipation of you entering me, being so big, makes my pussy drool with its warm cream.

I quiver with that thought.

I give in—I give in as your eyes go low, and you touch my face pulling it to yours and our lips touch with such a surge of electricity, that both our bodies jerk from it.

"Shittttt!!" we both say, as we pull back from each other and stare into our eyes.

You pull me to you again, as I try to back away; the feeling is too intense for me. Our lips softly touch again; you slide your hands down my shoulders as I hold my hands pressed against your chest.

Kissing each other deeply, your hands slide down to my waist, pulling me closer; I try to push away but you quickly slide your hands down to my round-firm ass and scoop me up into your body. I grow faint, and as I start to fall from weakened knees and your deep passionate kisses. You scoop me up again with your strong hands gripping my ass even firmer, still kissing me, causing me to cum right there in your arms.

You kiss my neck and gently bite it, as I claw into your shoulders trying to hold onto you, I then wrap my arms around your neck; you pick me up by my ass and I wrap my legs around your waist while our kisses become deeper and more intense.

You begin to pull my lips with your lips, and I can feel the thickness of your shaft pressed against my pussy, pulsating, warm, and jerking as you grind into me slowly—moaning.

The rain is pouring down all around us, and knowing that I am afraid of thunder and lightening, it makes the moment even more intense.

Our moans and sighs grow louder; "Ooooh shit baby" we both say at the same time, as we kiss and grind into each other; my legs loosen and I slide down your legs to stand—barely able to.

I try to back away from your kisses to catch my breath and you press your body into me more, grabbing my breasts and pinching my nipples, while I drown into the feeling of you. I gather enough strength to push back away from you, or did I, maybe you released me willingly, to prepare for your next move.

I stand there in your rain-drenched shirt, and it clings to me like a crazed lover, with my nipples fully erect, licking your taste and the rain from my lips. You stare at me hungrily, slowly pulling down your pants, and exposing the massiveness of your shaft.

You grab it hard into your hand, then begin to stroke it as you slowly walk towards me. I weaken as I stare at you, and the thickness of what you want to give to me—I could not move.

You grab me by my hair, pulling my head back, and my face up to yours, then you kiss me with deep kisses, all while stroking your hard thickness.

I stand there, helpless, defenseless, and dazed by the feeling. You step back away from me and stand there just looking, still stroking yourself, and say, "Take the shirt off baby!" I cannot move; you ask me again, and still; I stand there looking into your eyes; looking at your shaft as you stroked it—I was frozen.

You walk to me, staring into my eyes, then reach for my breasts, squeezing them, then suddenly you grab me by the shirt and rip it open. The buttons from it tear away from the material and shoot across the yard, then you pull it back and down past my shoulders roughly; yanking it, exposing my big breasts, small waist, curvy hips, and my swollen-waxed pussy.

Still standing there, almost in shock from what you had done, I could not distinguish my own wetness from the pouring rain.

You stand back from me again, pumping your thick shaft into your angry fist, looking at me in all of my nakedness while I began to shiver, and my breasts began to bounce.

"Mmmmm . . . baby, I am going to make you feel so good!" You say, still stroking it as the rain taps onto the head of it.

"Did you hear me baby?" You said intensely. I did hear you, but the feeling of it all was so euphoric that I could not respond. It was so intense, so surreal that I wanted to, but could not do anything but stand there and feel the feeling of the moment.

I wanted you, I wanted you to take me badly, and to do whatever you wanted to do to me. I wanted to feel whatever it was that you wanted to make me feel, and just allow myself to feel it. So I continued to stand there, and let you gaze at my body while you pumped your thick shaft into your fist.

As I stared into your eyes, I mumbled nervously, "I want you baby, I want whatever you want to give to me!" as I began to pull the shirt down past my elbows.

You approached me quickly, grabbing me suddenly, "No baby, don't take it all the way off, the white against your skin drives me crazy!" You then lean down and take my nipple into your mouth, nibbling it, sucking it, clinching it between your teeth; while looking up into my face.

I grab you by the hair and push your face into the thickness of my breasts, then deep into my cleavage while your hands grasp the smallness of my waste.

You moan a deep growling noise, and slowly slide your hands to the small of my back, then down to my ass cheeks, pulling them apart, squeezing them with your big thick hands, and I cum so hard that I feel my feet begin to slip on the grass.

"Aaaaaaah, you like that baby, don't you?" you say, as you look up into my face, licking my big firm breasts like they were ice cream, then trailing your tongue underneath my chin to my mouth and kiss my lips wet, juicy, and deep.

I can barely hear you, as the orgasm was so strong it caused my water-drenched ears to ring in a low tone. You stand up, then back away from me again, looking at me standing there helpless in the rain, shivering, as my nipples are so hard and thick, that they begin to hurt.

I walk slowly towards you on tip toes, with your shirt still hanging off of my elbows, and I kiss you, I kiss you deeply, then slide down to my knees to take you into my mouth, and before I part my lips, I look up at you; into your eyes, as the rain is falling down into my face, while you stand over me with your shaft still in hand, stroking it steadily.

"Do you want my mouth baby, do you want to feel it deep into my mouth and to the back of my throat?" I say as I remove your hands from it, while on my knees at your feet, still looking up at you, and letting the rain lubricate my lips, preparing to take your shaft into my wet mouth.

You look down at me with eyes wide as if to see it better, removing the hair from your face. I touch the tip of it with my tongue, and then kiss it; all while looking up at you, watching your head go back, with your face to the sky. I hold it in my hand, squeezing it, slowly stroking it, and teasing it. Mmmmm, I rub my tongue across the tip of it again, and you almost lose your balance.

"Yessss, this is what you want, this is how you want it from me right baby?" I say to you, as I lick you from the base of your shaft to the tip, and then take the head of it into my mouth, moaning and humming for you to feel the vibration. Tightening my lips tighter I squeeze it with my mouth as I swirl my tongue around it; all while looking up at you, watching the intensity on your face.

You reach down and grab the big clump of my hair, holding it tight in your fist, and began to pull my mouth deeper onto your shaft. As I struggle to take the choke, you growl out, "You're gonna have to learn to take it all baby!"

Gurgling and struggling to keep up with your strokes deeper into my mouth, I put my hands onto your waist to guide you to give me only what I could handle.

"Damn baby, that feels so good!!" You say, while I struggle with the choking feeling, still gurgling as my face pounds harder onto your throbbing shaft; the tears from my eyes soak into my rain-stained face, and my mascara begins to run down my cheeks.

The rain softens, almost to a mist, and you relax your body, letting go of my hair, resting your hands just above your ass, slowly grinding and pumping into my face, mumbling, "Oh my God, I do not want to come yet." Your voice softens as you slowly pull your shaft from the suction of my mouth.

"Mmmmm . . . Shit Baby" you say, as your legs begin to shake, while you are trying to straighten them. I gurgle, then swallow the mixture of your cream, and rain into my open mouth and fall onto my back, stretching my body out onto the wet warm grass.

I watch you standing there, with your face still pointed to the sky. One hand on your shaft, holding it, gripping it, trying to keep from cumming; watching my breasts rock slow in movement, and the rain puddle that is starting to form into my navel, and slide itself off the side of my waist.

Slowly I spread my legs, reaching down to rub my swollen pussy, waiting for you to enter me. I look at you smiling, as I tickle my fingers across my clit, then bring my knees up to the sky, and spread my legs even further apart.

You fall down on one knee still holding your shaft in your hand, clamping it tight to keep from cumming. You throw your head back towards the sky and holler into the air, "Shit, I don't want to cum yet baby!" I lie there smiling as the misty rain settles onto my body, caressing me like a thin blanket of lust.

Slowly, you insert two fingers into my pussy, watching it spread me apart and my back arches with pleasure. Mmmmm . . . I moan and grind into them, forcing you to put them into me even deeper.

I lift my legs into the air, rest the bottom of my feet onto your chest, rubbing my toes against your hard nipples—just then, the thunder starts, and my body shakes with fear causing you to slip into my softness with your thick throbbing shaft.

The rain starts to come down a little heavier now, as I close my eyes, lying there on the grass while you slowly push yourself deep inside of me.

The thunder crashes again, and my body begins to tremble with fear, as you plunge deeper into me while looking down into my face and my closed eyes feel up with rain.

"Mmmmm . . . Baby, this feels good huh?" You say, while you begin to tease me by inching yourself deeper into my tight little pussy, then stopping to watch me squirm and moan.

Trembling, I lift my feet past your shoulders, to lift my ass up from the wet grass, and you grab it and pull me closer to you, so that you can go deeper.

Damn your wet hands feel good gripping my ass, I thought, as the rain begins to thicken even more.

The thunder became more frequent, with sprigs of lightening, and my body began to tremble intensely. I could no longer open my eyes, the wind started to blow, and the sky darkened.

"We had better go inside baby", I said in a trembling voice, but you kept plowing deeper into me, gripping my ass, saying, "It is okay baby, we will be okay!!" Your strokes became deeper and more forceful.

This is crazy, I thought to myself, but it felt so damn good.

I try to turn sideways to turn onto my hands and knees, as you continued to pound me deep and deeper. You then aggressively turn me over to my belly, and I hiked my ass high into the air and it spread open to you, revealing my plump-swollen pussy as the rain trickled down the crevice of my ass; mixing with our juices.

You grab me by your shirt that is clinging to my back and yank me into you hard, and I feel your balls slam against my clit. Your shaft slips, then slide between my ass cheeks. Gasping with surprise and startled by the crackling of the thunder and the lightening that lit up the dark rainy sky; my body shook and quivered so bad that it caused you to plow into me like a madman—moaning and growling.

I look over my shoulder to see that you were looking down at it spreading my pussy open and watching my cream being washed away by the rain as you continued to plunge deeper and harder into me. You release your shirt, licking the rain from your lips, then grab my ass with both hands, still riding me hard.

You lean forward onto my back and reach your hand around my waist to rub my wet pussy while biting my back, causing me to have a string of intense orgasms that made my body fall away from your shaft.

Suddenly you stand, grab me by my waist, picking me up, and then guide me over to the sofa swing underneath the covered patio. I sit there on the swing trembling, shivering, and looking up at you with parted quivering lips, with eyes wide, smeared mascara; my wet hair stuck to my face, neck, and shoulders.

You stand there in front of me, looking down at my rain soaked body, stroking your hard, thick shaft into your fist.

You reach out your hand to my face lifting it up to look into your eyes, then slowly insert your thumb into my mouth. My quivering lips open willingly to your thumb pulling my bottom lip down and you rub it across the top of my bottom teeth, while cupping my chin.

"Oh shit baby—I want to cum in your sexy little mouth, just like this" I did not want you to—I was afraid, afraid because I had never done that before. I was afraid that I would not be able to handle it, afraid that it would be too much, and that it would not look or be as sexy as you wanted it to be.

You notice the look of concern on my face as you move closer to me, stroking yourself as you became even harder, saying, "It's okay baby, I will be gentle with you, you will like it, just relax okay?"

I lean forward a little, wrapping my plump lips around your thumb, sucking it, licking it, looking up into your face as you let go of your shaft to remove your hair from your face.

Instantly—I slip my mouth from your thumb onto the thickness of your shaft with a strong suction just on the tip of it. You jerk, looking down with all of your attention on my juicy wet lips wrapped around your throbbing pole, looking up at you with big eyes.

Wrapping both hands around your shaft, I suck the tip while jerking it hard, with my hand, to make you cum harder than you ever have before.

I massage your balls with one hand, tickling them, playing with them, until I began to taste the saltiness of your cum pumping its way into my mouth.

You begin to growl louder and louder, then grab a handful of my hair as you stroke your hard shaft slow and deep into my wet mouth. I begin to gag a little and try to pull away. "Relax baby, relax your mouth, relax your throat and let me in there." You say in a trembling and reassuring voice. I begin to relax as you stroke your stiffness slow and deep, then deeper into my mouth touching the back of my throat.

I relax and begin to go with the rhythm that you are forcing me to by holding handfuls of my hair. I reposition myself on the swing, and prepare for you to cum. With your head all the way back, you grab me by the hair and head with both hands and thrust a little faster, and a little deeper into my mouth. I let go of your shaft to put my hands onto your waist, to keep you from going too far into my throat.

You let go of my hair with one hand and grab your hard pulsing shaft, stroking it while you grind into my mouth, then pulling me by my hair onto it.

"Yeah baby", you say calmly as you look down at my quivering lips trying to take all of you into the back of my throat, making muffled gurgling sounds, struggling to keep up with your strokes.

I felt it jerk and then tighten. "Are you ready baby, I am going to cum, and I want you to swallow me, I want you to swallow every last drop."

My throat instantly tightens and I begin to gag and choke; losing the rhythm of your strokes. "Oh shit baby, relax, come on; relax." You say in a soft and gentle voice, but it is too late, because all I could think about is your hot cum gushing into my mouth, filling it up and then choking.

You slow down, throbbing, pulsing, hard, so hard I could feel every vein of it with my tongue, then I relax and our rhythm is matched again.

We both begin to moan as I reach down to rub my pussy while taking you deep into my mouth, and as I begin to cum, you scream out, "I'm going to fucking cum baby, yessss, keep sucking it, just like that!"

Your orgasm was coming in a rage, as you pound your hard shaft deeper into my mouth, and I took it, sucking it, licking it, squeezing it with my mouth, on the edge of cumming myself.

You grab my head with both hands pounding deep into my mouth then scream out loud, "Here it comes baby!!!" You shoot it deep to the back of my throat just as I was cumming and my throat opened to receive it. You shoot again, and it fills my mouth and begins to pour out onto my breasts, then dripping down onto my pulsating pussy.

You pull it from my mouth and shoot it onto my lips and face, squeezing it hard with one hand and holding a hand full of my hair with the other, as you looked down into my face.

You shoot again, all over my big breasts while they jiggle and my body quake and quiver from the rage of my own orgasm, and my juices squirt out onto your leg and foot.

I begin to scream, "Oh shit baby" while your cum still drips from my mouth, down to my big breasts, and into my hand that rubbed my swollen-squirting pussy.

"OH . . . FUCK . . . BABY!!! THAT WAS SO FUCKING GOOD, YOU WERE SO DAMN HOT!!!" You holler out into the air, as the last of your cum shoots onto my bottom lip and chin then leaks down your shaft.

Breathing deep and hard as I fall forward, almost falling off of the swing; you place one hand on my back leaning over me to let down the back of the swing into a bed.

You lay me back onto it, walk into the bedroom, grab a towel, and the oversized comforter off of the bed, wipe my body down, then climb onto the swing and nestle up behind me.

As you pull the comforter onto our bodies, you whisper into my ear. "It is crazy how the rain turns us into such wild animals." As you give me soft sensual kisses to my ear.

I push my round ass into your drooling softness, smiling as you make the swing rock, then putting your arm around my waist to hold me tight.

Both of us pressed into each other, breathing heavily, listening, and watching as the storm rages all around us.

We fall asleep, sticky, wet, and warm—in the rain.

THE DOCTOR'S OFFICE

I scurry into the doctor's office, running late, fumbling with my briefcase, unbuttoning my suit jacket, and turning off my cell phone, as I approached the counter to sign in.

I could smell your cologne, it was so arousing to my senses, that it caused me to suddenly stop and look around the waiting room, and there you sat, looking at me, and I suddenly became flush at how very sexy you looked in your white dress shirt, jeans and square-toed dress shoes.

I quickly gathered myself, took a deep breath, then turned slowly around, scanning the room for a seat, wanting to sit far away from you, but close enough to where we could see each other.

In finding the perfect seat, I remove my jacket, lay it across the back of the chair, trying not to look at you, but feel you looking at me.

I sit down, cross my legs, grab a magazine and pretend to look at it, but I was really looking at you. It was like I could feel the heat coming off of your body, radiating towards me.

Something about your eyes and the look on your face, when you looked at me entering the room, caught my attention, as well as the intoxicating smell of your cologne. Everyone in the waiting room could tell that there was a strong sexual tension between us.

Fumbling through the magazine, I could feel you staring at me, as if to stared deep into my soul. Then thinking that you may have been looking at someone behind me, I turned to look, and there was no one there. I turn back; you smile and look down into your book—I looked away blushing.

I became nervous, as I glanced up from my magazine to look at you again, to study you closely, your eyes, your mouth, the hair on your chest and arms, then closing my eyes to embed you deep into my memory—into my taste.

I open them to see that you shifted your body, exposing to me your strong arms, hands, and thick thighs. You thumb through your book, then glance my way again, and I feel my nipples harden to greet your eyes as you scan my body with precision—I am liking this game.

A coy smile creeps to the corner of my mouth; licking my lips, I watch you as you watched me. Feeling the intense sexual energy between us, I bite my lip and shift in my seat, to cross my long chocolatety legs as my skirt lifts showing you the very edge of my thigh-high stockings.

You become uncomfortable now, shifting constantly in your seat, as your shaft begins to grow, feeling the pressure of it being constricted in your jeans. You try to adjust yourself unnoticed; clearing your throat, struggling to keep your eyes fixed on what you were reading—finding it difficult to do so.

I unbutton two of the top buttons on my blouse, exposing just a hint of my massive cleavage; I close my eyes again, taking you in, breathing deep; with your cologne filling my nostrils, and trying not to explode into an orgasm, as my body begins to quake—to quiver.

Mmmmm . . . I think to myself how yummy you are, so stimulatingly delicious that I am starting to lose control. I can feel my panties become moist and my nipples are so hard now, that they lift the material of my bra away from my firm round breasts.

Watching your eyes become large, you begin to slowly lick your lips, I close mine again, uncrossing, then crossing my legs, as my high heel loosens from my foot, then dangles from the tip of my toes.

I feel nothing but sheer ecstasy, as a coating of sweat blankets my body, while the patients all around us in the waiting room find it hard not to watch.

I open my eyes to see that you are watching me intensely, lowering your eyes, leaning back in your seat, with your legs apart, then sliding lower into the chair, making me see your erection through your pants. My eyes open wide, and a gasp escapes my lips, alerting others to look at me, then you, then look away.

I panic as my orgasm that I held back from the time I looked into your eyes, starts to overtake my body. I slid to the edge of my chair, quickly lifting the magazine from my lap, and held it in front of my face to hide myself from everyone in the waiting room as I began to cum so hard, and trying not to scream, I bit into my lip, tasting my own blood.

It was so strong, I tore the magazine in half, right down the middle, eking out a small whimpering cry, while others in the room tried not to look, but could not help it.

We both looked at each other through the torn magazine that I still held in front of my face in disbelief. I was paralyzed with fright, as their faces slowly turned away in anger, with chatter, with shock, alarm, giggles, and some with the lust of our moment.

Suddenly, the nurse opened the door and called out my name. I gathered my things, placed the torn magazine on the table, walked embarrassingly over to you and gave you a soft juicy wet kiss on your lips, smiled, then asked; "Honey, do you want to pick up carryout for dinner tonight? Or would you like for me to pick it up on my way home?"

Everyone in the waiting room looked at us in confusion, as we smiled into each other's eyes.

I turn away from you, then walked through the door, and before I disappeared down the hallway, I looked back at you, you winked your eye to me, and blew me a kiss, then told everyone that it was okay, that I was your girl; you then raised your book to your face and continued reading—smiling.

LIKE CHOCOLATE

I sat there scanning the room, looking into the smiling and laughing faces that surrounded me, and that is when I saw him.

He was brown skinned, evenly toned choco-latte, blended with a hint of crème, a hint of cinnamon, a taste of vanilla, and a shot of Cheyenne pepper.

Ooooh he was chilled, he was spicy, yet smooth, with a tempting tantalizing air about him, my eyes were locked in surprise, locked in lust, locked into wanting that tall drink of Ooooh Weeee.

I am finding it hard to look away, but tore myself from him to contain the tigress that I felt raging inside of myself.

My skin began glowing a reddish brown, a coating of lusty sweat that covered my arms, breasts and face, it was apparent to all around me, that I was aroused, and truthfully? I did not give a damn!

He had something I wanted, something that I needed, just thinking of what his voice may sound like, what he would feel like and make me feel, caused me to stir even more.

Damn, I need to collect myself, he's making me come undone, making me so wet that I feel my cream seeping through my panties, wetting my inner thighs.

I uncross and cross my legs, trying to pull it all together, clearing my throat, and took a sip of my drink that tasted dreamy like the dreams I seen in him—which—takes me back to him.

I could almost hear music when I looked at him, even though there was music humming low—sinking itself into his background.

What I could hear was a jungle beat, a primitive beat, one that had a strong gravitational pull that pulled me to him, straight into him.

Something about him caused me to stir deep inside of myself; I lowered my face in shame and embarrassment, then raise my posture slowly and sat my drink to the countertop.

I see his back, so wide that it would put a cobra to shame, as it spreads open and down into a tapered waistline of his nice toned ass.

Dammit, who is he, and how can I get to know him, to be in his world, to maybe be his girl!!

I try to silence all the music and the chatter around me, to focus on his voice as I watch his mouth move in almost slow motion. I zone in and can hear nothing, but suddenly noticing his large hands that cup his drink, and his thick long fingers that seemingly wrapped around his glass—twice.

I gasp . . . and I gasp again when noticing his thick wrists that strongly attached to his long toned arms. I look away, I look away out of respect that he may be taken—shit—he have me shaken!!!

He stands there, across the room, slightly angled to where I can see just enough of him. To see that he is handsome, not one of those metro-sexual guys, he was a man, a real man, a handsome man that reminded me of a smooth piece of chocolate, melting in my mouth, causing me to drown in the flavor, the smoothness, the richness of him.

Mmmmm . . . I could almost feel his taste—in my mouth.

Sitting back in frustration, I drown into him with fantasies of him bending me over, leaning over my body with his big hands gripping my soft round ass, as he push into me—hard; leaning forward to whisper into my ear words of his jungle passion, thrusting to touch the bottom of me, the tightness of me, the end of me, the all of me—Shit!!

I sip again my drink, then close my eyes to see him more clearly, to feel him inside of me, gripping me, biting at my neck and pulling my hair.

My breathing intensifies, as I squeeze the coldness of my drink on the brink of a monumental orgasm, and with opening my eyes to a squint in his direction, he is gone; but—but I came anyway, cumming so hard that I rocked the chair, clearly stifling all that were around me; gritting my teeth, puckering my lips to keep from screaming aloud, and at that moment, he was there, standing beside me, placing his large hand in the small of my back; whispering his deep voice into my ear, lips brushing lightly with warmth, and a sensual feel that caused my body to tremble into a rage of multiple orgasms.

Barely able to catch my breath, gasping in total surprise, and trembling intensely, I whisper into his face—my name is . . .

Then he leans in towards me and kissed me softly into silence,

with lips . . .

that taste like . . .

warm . . .

Chocolate.

I LIKED IT THOUGH

He pushed me backwards onto his bed fully clothed, not softly, not like in a lover's dream where you float like a feather falling in slow motion, landing perfectly and every hair falls into place; it was rough!

But I liked it though—Huh!

He dove on top of me like a wrestler, almost knocking the breath from me, as he pressed his lips against mine, grinding his hardness into me and me grinding back, but his kisses. His kisses were so tender it made me forget the way I landed onto his soft bed!

Mmmmm . . . But I was liking it though.

He lifts himself above me gazing into my face intensely with his piercing blue eyes, straddling me, still grinding and pulling my hair hard away from my face, and holding it there, while staring into my eyes as I began to feel the pressure—the pain!

But damn . . . I liked it though. Shit!!!

He unzips my sweater, revealing my swollen bouncing breasts, and leans down to kiss them—then my stomach. He slides down onto his knees, landing smoothly to the floor, as he unzips my low-rise jeans revealing my panties, kissing right above them, causing me to shutter!

And "Ooooh Shit—I liked it though.

I lift my ass up off of his bed while he slowly pulls down my jeans, revealing my long chocolate legs, then he nibbles at my thighs. Mmmmm . . . I cover my wet pussy with my hand, but the scent of it drove him mad, as he yanks my heels and jeans off, flinging them across the room!

Ooooh shit, did I feel freaky—but I was liking it though.

He quickly removed his shoes, shirt, and pants as his long, thick, hard, throbbing shaft, angrily popped out of his underwear, and seeing it for the first time—I could not move. It was thick, tight, lurching and ready to enter my tight sweet spot. I was scared!

But I liked it though. Mmmmm . . . Hmmmm . . . (Giggle) (Smile)

We both stood facing each other, at the foot of his bed, looking into each others eyes, as we slowly took off the last of our clothing and I could hardly breathe as we kissed each other's lips and feeling each other's body—we climbed slowly into his bed.

And I am still liking it though.

He laid me softly onto my back, looking deep into my eyes, and began to kiss my neck, burying his face deep into the crease of it.

He inhales my skin and I hear him mumble that he likes the way I smell, and how soft my skin felt to his touch; it made my body quiver and my legs part slowly.

I take a long deep breath as he begins to enter me . . . and I, Ooooh Shittttt . . .

It's too big though!!!

(To Be Continued . . .)

I MISS YOU

Lying in the middle of my bed with my hands placed on the flattened part of my belly, feeling the breathing of my breaths. Breathing slow and deep as I close my eyes and drown deep into my thoughts of you.

As I—wait for you.

Thinking about the softness of your lips when they touch mine, how they cause me to sink into you, and when they clash into our moments of ecstasy; causing us to grab at each other's clothing, at each other's soft moist skin; wrestling into each other's feel.

My belly sinks even lower feeling my pulse pounding harder from my heart into my stomach, allowing my hands to capture the beat of it into the center of my palms. This—is what you make me feel with just the thought of you.

I lift my head to reposition it on the pillow, shifting my body to become more comfortable into the feel of my soft bed; closing my eyes for a moment to see you, to see you in my minds eye, to taste you, to smell the smell of your skin when it begins to perspire with your lust that builds from you seeing me, touching me, feeling me—kissing me the way that you kiss me.

I slide my hands up from my belly to feel my rib cage, feeling my soft skin that cushions each bone that secures my heart from breaking away to attach itself to yours. I tell myself to breathe, to breathe deep and release it into the night's air that surrounds me. I—am missing you.

You use to touch me so softly, tickling me to laughter, girly giggles, and smiles, as we rolled around on the floor in front of a television that was on, but never watched.

Watching the light from it reflect and dance off of our bodies as we stopped to stare into each other's eyes and you touch my face, then we—kissed.

I remember how your hands would tremble as you pulled my blouse from my shoulder to kiss the outer edge of my collarbone. Slowly trailing your lips to my neck, then to my lips, as they trembled to kiss me with a passionate kiss, making my body quiver.

Mmmmm . . . I remember this, and your eyes. Your eyes that left a mark on my soul like a tattoo never to fade.

Lying there wondering what I will say, what I will do when I see you again. Wondering if there will be words, if our feelings will be the same when our eyes meet.

I lift myself to get dressed, as the butterflies dance in my stomach, causing my body to moisten with a lusty glow from thinking of you. I can no longer control it. I am wanting you—so bad. Right now!

Walking to my closet, I stand in front of the mirrored doors in just my underwear, fresh out of the shower, all oiled up; starring at myself.

Wondering if you will like this lacey matching set that I chose to wear just for you. Thinking about how you always said that it never mattered what I wore, even if it was just nakedness and a smile—I smile.

I stand there touching my belly feeling the butterflies of what this night will be like when our eyes meet again. Will you make me weak in the knees? Will I cause you to stutter your words as you stare into my eyes, my face, with glances to my body, watching my lips nervously pucker?

I pick out the little black dress, simple, but elegant, and slip into my black heels, as I clip my earrings to my lobes, staring at myself as your car pulls up in front of the house, I turn from the mirror quickly with excitement, smiling, and my body shivers with the thought of your touch.

I wait patiently while you walk to the door, not wanting to appear overly excited, I wait for you to ring the doorbell, and there is nothing. I wait, there is nothing. I wait—still nothing. I begin to panic, wondering, waiting, shaking, thinking, with pounding heart and frantic butterflies that are losing their rhythm of panic.

It rings—and I melt.

Approaching the door with a wispy stride, I see your shadow as you turn and I open the door for you. You stand there, looking into my eyes, as I stood and looked into yours, not a beat lost from the last time we saw each other, I could tell by the way you were looking at me, and I could feel the heat from my body jump onto yours, and yours onto mine, neither one of us could move.

Smiling—and blushing.

I step back from the doorway to welcome you in, as you walked over the threshold, not taking your eyes off of my eyes. You tower past me as the butterflies danced a happy dance in my belly then flew outside the door, into the night.

In closing the door, you finally say hello, with a smile that lit up both of our faces, and smiling back into your face with a nervous reply, you hand me flowers; our fingers touched and sparked off a bright light of electricity from the hotness that we generated for each other.

I look away, trying to control my lusty expressions of wanting to feel your lips to mine, I cannot help but to look at you, and you knew, as I knew, that there was no way we could get through the evening in a public place—not tonight.

You look at me, and with one step, you are standing in front of me and I look up into your face as you grab me tight, and I feel the familiar tremble of your hands and you feel the familiar quiver of my body, as our eyes stare into each other's. Lowering your face to mine you kiss me a kiss of juicy lips that caused me to feel faint, and I begin to fall away from you.

Quickly you scoop me up by my ass, kissing me with wet sensual kisses of I miss you, I need you, I want you right now, and I cannot catch my breath.

My knees weaken and I find myself clawing at your shoulders to hold on, trying to breathe. Kissing the juiciness of your lips, I pull away, wanting to look into your face, to open my eyes to feel this feeling deeply that you are planting inside of me.

Pushing me against the wall you pull my dress from my shoulders to kiss my neck, and I become dizzy with you, with your touch, losing my balance, kicking off my shoes as you unzip my dress, and it falls to the floor.

You intertwine my fingers into yours, and place them above my head, kissing me with soft wet kisses that cause my juices to fill my panties.

Holding both my hands above my head with your large hand, you loosen your belt to remove your pants with the other. I . . . am . . . ready . . . for you.

Breaking free to lift your shirt above your head, I expose your sexy chest, sprinkled with hair that peppered your thick hard nipples and trickled down into the waistband of your boxer briefs to disappear just beneath them.

I have missed you, I am needing you, I am wanting you, is what my body is screaming; melting me as we slow our actions and step away from each other as I slide slowly down the wall, to the floor with my lipstick smeared across my face.

Dropping to your knees, you pull me hard away from the wall by my ankles, and I let you.

You pull my panties off, and I let you.

You spread my legs apart, and I let you.

You lower your face to my pussy, and I let you.

Sniffing me deep, closing your eyes to embed the smells of me into your nostrils—and I—let you.

Your lips kiss it, then . . . kiss it again, and again while looking into my eyes. I feel the warmth of your wet tongue stirring into my juiciness, sucking and tasting my peach as my body begins to vibrate with the coming of me cumming.

Lifting yourself from me, licking my taste from your lips . . . hovering over me . . . staring into my eyes I can smell the earthiness of my pussy on your mouth as you lean down to kiss me while slowly sliding yourself into me and I drown into the pleasure of it.

Feeling you.

Feeling you deeper than I ever felt you before.

Feeling my tightness to the point of splitting, feeling that painful pain of pleasure, as your eyes roll to the back of your head and you sink deep, and deeper into me, mumbling.

Mumbling words of intense pleasure; softly, steadily, opening me, sinking my nails into your shoulders as you drop to rest your hairy chest onto my slow . . . bouncing . . . breasts.

Whispering your lusty words into my ear, tracing your lips and warm breath to my lobe, slowly thrusting inside and out of me.

Trembling, I wrap my legs around your waist and my arms around your back, letting you know that I want all of you.

Everything—

Everything that you want to give to me—

Give it to me!

Your strokes begin to quicken, as you sink your face into the crease of my neck, biting me lightly, moaning, as I moan into whimpering cries of pain and pleasure.

Our pace quickens as I fill you thicken inside me, spreading me, splitting me, slamming yourself deep into my pussy, grinding me, fucking me like I dreamed that you would—just like this.
Like now!

My orgasms take over my body, not one, not two, not three, there were many and tears begin to roll from the corners of my eyes, as I close them and let you take me, to feel me, to want me, to miss me, as you cum inside of me with a loud growl of extreme pleasure, of quaking body, gritting teeth, holding me tight, as our hearts pound the same hard beat, almost touching, connecting through the strong vibration of us cumming, as we came!!

Breathing now . . .

Just breathing . . .

Feeling you throb inside of me . . .

Feeling you, touching you while my tears flow freely . . .

Kissing you . . .

Cinda "Cin" Cianelli

Holding you tight into my arms and me into yours . . .

Just breathing . . .

Feeling our hearts pounding in silence . . .

Bodies sweating . . .

Lips kissing each other's wet skin . . .

I Missed You!

CALL TO ME

Everything is pointing me to you. Calling to me in my dreams deep into the night, causing me to thrust my pelvic forward while sleep holds me in its grip.

Your arms open wide welcoming me into the folds of your strength, with swirls of brushed hair, warming me with tickles of lust; filling me till my cup runneth over.

I—sigh.

Clearly . . .
I hear you through your whispers of soft trembling voice and my round full breasts race toward you, to touch chest to nipples bouncing into heat.

My eyes close, and open to the feel of your all that you want to give to me.

Feeling it rise between my thighs, throbbing as it pounds hot blood to thicken as it thickens.

Breath . . .
Breathing into chilled air, escaping with clouds of erotic steaming dreams, closed eyes touching, grasping into tightening grips.

You . . .
You call to me in silence and sweet sounds of breathing deep; releasing into echoes of moaning, wetting my walls of ecstasy, dripping with my sweet honey through the valley of my swollen peach.

Cupping my wide hips into spreading legs. Grinding of motions opening into dizziness, to catch moments of intensity that darken the skies with thunderous storm clouds and flashing blades of light to explode my juices down the roundness of my ass!!!

Lazily I drip drops of you onto my warm wet sheets.

Feeling you call to me.

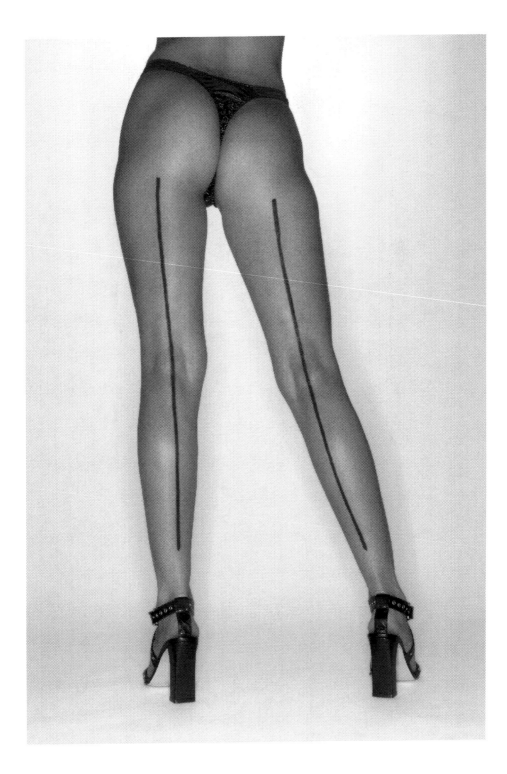

I LIKE

I like.

I like it when you touch me like that, touching me right there, and there, and there too.

Touching me with your rough hands, lightly tracing my soft skin with shaky fingertips as you stare deep into my eyes like that.

I like when you touch my hair, twirling each strand sending jolts of pleasure to those sensual parts of me, as if each strand specifically controls the heat, the fire, the desire, that burns deep inside of myself, causing my body to come alive and crave your touch.

I like when you touch my face then my lips like that. Tracing them with your fingertips and eyes, as I slowly part them for you to insert them into my wet mouth—just like that.

Mmmmm . . . And I like when you grab me around my waist like that, and forcefully pull me into you, causing me to gasp and submit myself to you, releasing to the pleasures that you make me feel.

Yessss . . . I like when you touch me there, there, and there too.

Touching my breasts then squeezing the roundness of them like that. Gripping my nipples in between your fingers then into your mouth like that, feeling the wetness of your tongue as it licks the hardness of them—just like that.

I like!

I like it when your hand slides down the center of my body like that, down to my navel feeling me quiver with anticipation, with wanting you, with wanting more of you—wanting you deep inside of me.

I like when you touch me there, there, and there.

I like how your hand begins to tremble as you slowly and hesitantly slide it from my navel down to my pussy like that, and my back arches away from the bed, and you lift yourself above me and kiss me with juicy wet kisses.

I like!

I like feeling my head spin and the blood rush from my head down to my pussy as it begins to swell like that. Just from knowing that your fingers are nearing it. I like these feelings that you make me feel and I like how you touch me there, there, and there too.

I like how you lower your body on top of mine like that, feeling the weight of it pressing down with a heaviness that causes me to melt into breathlessness, into chocolate—just like that.

I like when I feel the hardness of your shaft slide between my moist thighs, almost touching my pussy like that. While you push your arm through the small space between my back and the bed, pulling me to you like that, into you like that, wanting me just like that.

I like when you touch me there, there, and right there.

I like when I can feel your wetness seeping from your shaft, causing you to slip and slide shining my inner thighs with your warm slippery juices melting into mine like that.

Dammit!!! I like it when you touch me there, and there, and like that.

I like when you feel my heat, the heat that I feel from just looking at you like that, looking at your thick shaft that stands tall like the empire state building. And I like how it calls out to me like that, calling to me with that throbbing rage of desire.

Yessss—I like!

I like how you part my legs with your knees like that; gazing intensely into my eyes, giving me soft wet kisses, as I feel your warmth slowly opening me like that, parting me like that, spreading me, slowly sliding deep into my wetness—just like that.

Mmmmm . . . I like this feeling of me wanting to . . . Fuck you . . . Like that.

Yessss—Just like that!

Feeling your thick shaft pushing and pulsating deep into my wet pussy, feeling it to the bottom like that, touching the depth of me like that; causing me to gasp with pain, then a sudden pleasure of feeling you thicken inside of me.

Ooooo I like!

I like hearing the air escape it as you plunge deep and deeper like that, as I lift my legs to wrap them around your waist like that, and you reach your hands down to slide them underneath my ass like that, gripping and positioning me right where you want me.

Yessss—Like that!

I like the growling that comes from your throat, and the mumbling of your words into my ear like that, as we sync to each other's rhythm.

I—Like!

I like when you touch me there, there, and right there, and like that!

Liking the earthy smells of us grinding into each other like that!

Sweating like that!

When you fuck me like that!

Suck me like that!

Lick my pussy like that!!

Make my body jerk like that!!

Squirt like that.

I like when you make me Ooooo . . . like that!!

And Aaaaah—Like that!!

Cum so hard just like that!!

I—LIKE!!!

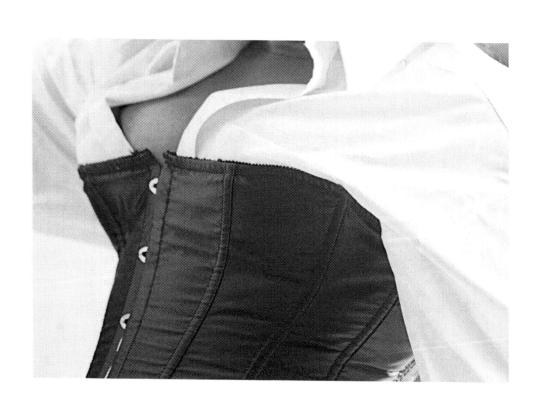

IN THE DARK

I waited up all night for you to come home from work; I cooked a nice light meal, even put candles on the table, and you did not even call.

I drank too much of the red wine that we were going to have with our dinner, and the sexy see-through, white lace dress and thongs were no longer sexy to me—on me.

I sat quietly, in the dinning room with my legs crossed up on the table, and my high heels dangling from my feet, wondering what could have kept you from me.

I poured another glass, watching my cell phone to see if it would light up with a message from you saying that you would be home shortly, that your meeting had ran into overtime—there was nothing.

No ring, no buzz, no light to bring my phone to life, to bring me back to life.

I sipped a little more of the wine, removing a couple of the hairpins from my hair, while watching the fire place burn in a bright orange light. I sipped again and decided to light the candles that sat on the table, waiting for us to share the flame of them together.

I waited, and waited and sipped again.

Something about the flickering candle light, and the fireplace caused me to become aroused, as I moved one foot from the table, to the floor; I looked down at my shape, thinking to myself, he is missing all of this, my soft round ass, my swollen breasts, my long legs, my thighs, my juicy moist lips and the feel of my mouth.

With that thought, I aroused myself even more, thinking of previous heated love sessions that we have had.

Instantly, my juices oozed into my panties as I grabbed for my breast, squeezing it while I took another sip of the wine. "How could you miss out on all of this baby?" I whispered to myself.

With both feet planted onto the floor now, I slide downward onto the edge of the chair and slowly open my legs, imagining that you are right there between them, and I quiver.

I take another sip of my wine, then grab both my breasts and squeeze them, pushing them together to touch each other, as I look down at the massive cleavage that I have caused—I shutter with excitement.

I lean my head down, stick my tongue out and begin to lick the tight roundness of them, I laugh out loud, and take another sip, realizing that I am getting a little carried away.

"Where could you be baby?" I ask aloud; as I sit up, then reach for the bottle to pour myself another.

I then lean back into the chair again, as my hand falls into my lap, landing on my pussy. Mmmmm . . . that was nice, I thought.

I lift up my ass and pull the lace dress upward past my hips to expose the white thongs that were so moist; you could see the shininess of my juices on my inner thighs. I pull my panties to one side to expose my massively swollen clit, protruding from my peach like a flower.

It surprised me to see it like that, and in being surprised, it started to throb, like a heartbeat and I could see it twitching.

The hair on my arms stood up, and I became more alert, more aware of what my body was feeling, what it was craving.

"I need you baby", I said aloud, as I clamped it between my fingers.

"Aaaaawwwww Shit!" I gasp with pleasure, as the echo of my voice bounced off the walls and awakened my senses even more.

"I wish you were here baby", I said in a muffled voice as I felt my juices slowly oozing down my ass, and puddle to the chair.

With every deep breath, my body shook, and the candles flickered, almost putting themselves out. I pull the lace dress down around my shoulders and underneath my breasts, causing them to sit up even perkier than usual, and my nipples hardened like never before, so hard that they began to ache. The moment had gotten so intense; I could almost smell your cologne in the air.

I closed my eyes, and pinched my nipples between my fingers again, causing my back to arch away from the chair. My body began to glow with perspiration from the warmth of the fireplace. I reach to remove more hair pens from my hair, letting it fall over my face as some of the strands stick to my lipstick.

"Ooooh baby, I wish you where here right now." I sip another sip of the wine, as I watched the candles on the table dance with my heavy breathing.

"Where are you, I need you so bad!!!"

As the candle wax began to slide down itself, it made me think of your cum, when you feel the warmth and squeeze of my mouth around your shaft.

Aaaauuugh, I cannot take it any longer, I need you inside of me right now!!!!!"

Just then, my words blew out the candle that sat closest to me, and the smell of it burning out caused me to erupt with an orgasm. "Ooooo Shittttt!!!!!!"

My eyes go low, as I continue to slowly rub my moist, and swollen, pussy.

With the room partially dark now, I remove the candlestick from its holder. "Damn baby, I can smell you, I want you so bad!" I lower it to my lap and begin to rub it across my clit, sinking deeper into the chair to where my ass is no longer mounted to it.

I rub the candlestick intensely across my clit, grinding my hips as I approach another earth-shattering orgasm.

The room starts to spin as the wine goes to my head and I cum so hard that my legs begin to tremble, calling out your name, as if you were right there with me.

Shittttt baby, damn.

In my drunken haze, I reach across the table and pull the lit candle towards me. The light from it sensually reflects off of my wet skin. I pull the top of my dress down to my waist, as I grab the lit candle from the table and hold it way above my body, allowing the wax to drip down onto my breasts.

Aaawwwww Shittttt, that feels so good, I rub my pussy slowly, as it swells in my hand. I dripped the wax onto my nipples, my arms, my face, and my lips—sealing them shut.

I reach for the other candlestick and rub it across my clit, and while the candle wax continues to drip onto my body, I slowly insert the candlestick into my wetness and came so hard that the sound of my voice seemed to be coming from within my ears, as the wax had my lips completely sealed.

I could smell you even more now, and the cologne you wear arouses me to another orgasm. I stand and lean over the table, still stroking myself with the candlestick, I put the other out, afraid of catching the tablecloth on fire.

In doing so, I suddenly feel the roughness of your hands on my round ass, my body shakes with fear and excitement, as I look back and it is you; completely nude, gazing at me with those sexy eyes.

You take the candlestick from my hand, as I brace myself onto the table. You stroke my pussy with it, slowly, in and out, while lightly biting my back; my body jerks hard with the feeling and excitement of it all. I muffle a mixture of sighs and screams as my voice tries to break through the thick hardened wax.

I feel your stiff erection pressing between my ass cheeks, sliding up and down in the moisture that oozed from my pussy. You remove the candlestick slowly as you bite my back, and wrap your arm around my waist, pulling me towards you—I brace myself.

You whisper into my ear, "You want this baby, you want all of me inside of you?"

At this point, how could I say no? How could I be angry with you, how could I resist, and knowing that you stood in the shadows watching me get myself off all that time.

My pussy oozed more juices with that thought of you standing in the shadows watching me toy with myself. My body jerks intensely as I feel you reach for your thick throbbing shaft and probe for my sweet spot.

Mmmmm . . . I moan as you find the swollen opening and my juices greet you with a slipperiness that allowed you to spread me open and enter my tight pussy with ease.

I felt you lose your breath, as you stood up to look down at it enter me. The fire from the fireplace is in a rage as if to have become ignited from what was taking place.

I scream out in a muffled cry, as you slap my ass and it jiggles, both with the act of your hand hitting it, and your thrusts deep into me.

I reach my arms and hands behind me to lighten your push, trying to absorb your thrusts, but you quickly grab my wrists and hold them behind my back, using them as leverage to thrust even harder and heavier into me.

My cries are beyond muffled, as the wax loosens from the sweat of my face.

"Please baby!!!!!!!!!" "It is too big!!!!!" But you cannot hear me or do not want to hear me; you lunge forward, regaining your footing to thrust into me even harder.

"Oh My God Baby, Wait!!!!" But you still cannot hear me as you scan my body, looking at the candle wax slowly dropping from my moist skin.

The way that my dress was tightly wrapped, and bundled around my waist.

The way that my thong was pulled to the side, and the way that my pussy was so tightly wrapped around your shaft, that my juices left a circle of cream around it. In seeing all of this, it made you even more excited.

Your thrusts are full force now, as the table begins to shake and the table settings are smashing to the floor. You begin to growl in a low gruff tone, and speaking words that I do not understand, as I feel my juices sliding down my inner thighs.

"It hurts so good baby!!!" I say to you through clinched teeth.

You let go of my wrists and grab hold of my ass, thrusting like a madman, as I scream with pure pain and pleasure.

"I'm going to cum baby, I'm going to fucking cum in your tight little hole!!!!" You holler into the air as the bottle of wine rolls off the table and fall to the floor then puddles at our feet.

"Are you ready baby???" You say in a shaky, intense voice.

"Here it cums!!!!!!" Ooooh Fuck, your pussy is so tightttt!!!!!" You scream out uncontrollably.

Your thrusts are so intense, it is making that wet smacking sound that caused me to scream out, "Don't stop baby, I am going to cum, Oh My God!!!" I scream as my legs begin to shake with such an intensity that my pussy squeezed your shaft harder, sending you into another orgasm, and as I squirted my juices down our legs, as I erupted into a blinding orgasm; I felt you feel me up again with the hotness of your cum, as you slam your body onto my back, biting at my neck, breathing heavily.

We lie on the table, both of us sweating, panting, trembling, quivering, and shivering from our earth-shattering orgasms that we imposed onto each other.

Speechless, bodies wet, glistening in the firelight, trying to catch our breath; we lie there in silence breathing heavily, until a calmness fills the room, and you can hear only the crackling of the fire burning low in the fire place.

Then finally you say to me, "Baby, I was home all this time, the meeting ended early and I fell asleep in the basement watching TV with my earphones on, waiting for you to get home, and breathlessly, still lying on the table we both began to laugh.

UNTOUCHED

I fall asleep at night, only to dream of you.

I start by deeply focusing my thoughts, giving it my all, my everything; to make you come to me.

As I drift into the sweet ecstasy of my sleep, I can hear the softness of your voice sexing me, whispering to me; stroking my body with a familiar tenderness that awakens that part of me that has been sleeping for so long.

I first see your eyes, they come into focus so clearly, the shape of them alone proves that you are a very passionate kisser.

They call out to me, drowning and bathing me deep in all that I see in you, and what you want to give to me. My nipples become hardened, just by knowing this of you.

I wait patiently, breathlessly, watching intensely as you manifest yourself right before my eyes.

You walk towards me out of darkened shadows and smoke, almost gliding. Your nostrils twitch and flare opening wide in taking in the smells of my skin, the smells of my lust that sweats of a strong fiery passion.

You bury your nose deep into the crease of my neck, wrapping your arms around my waist, taking long slow whiffs of me. You become instantly aroused, but try to contain it. You then whisper to me—voice trembling, low and deep; "I want you, I want this, I want this to happen tonight".

Your lips are parted, and moist, anticipating that first kiss that will surely have me all a quiver. Shooting bolts of pleasure to that wet moist place that calls your name with such desire—only you can hear it.

I reach my fingers to your lips, to silence you before you speak again; to silence what you want from me, from what you want to tell me, just for a little while longer, and it slips past your lips, into your mouth and I feel your moist tongue swirl around it causing a jolt of electricity through my body; such a sudden surge of intense pleasure that it could light up an entire city.

Mmmmm . . . You awaken me, making me want you, making me crave you into sleepless nights of tangled sheets, whispering deep voices and moaning; penetrating the silence of my warm body with sweats of pure lust.

You awaken me, you awaken that fire that has become a raging flame; it is hard to contain; sunken so deep into my loins that I awake screaming your name, heaving breathes of orgasms of being untouched, and soaked in lust-wet sheets.

You begin to fade, and in panic, I awaken in drowsiness, lifting myself from my bed, only to remember that you are just a dream.

My room is dark with eyes focused on the clock across the room, I lay my head back onto my pillow, breathing the sighs of sex, as you fade in and out of focus, then slowly reappear.

Your tallness stifles me, as I move to stand, then you stand, and reach your hands around my waist, pulling me into you, pulling me in as I am but a fraction of your size, and your closeness causes me to tremble into your arms, feeling weak, as I look up into your face, into those deep passionate eyes.

The massiveness of your body, and the true girth that I feel throbbing against my pussy as you pull me closer, harder, and

79

tight into your arms, with eyes looking into mine, so sincere that I cannot help but to touch your face; pulling it to me for a soft warm kiss.

You pick me up and I wrap my legs around your thick waist and your strength is unmatched by all before you. I feel the bulge of your muscular arms and the thickness of your neck that sends me into such bliss that I close my eyes, pucker my lips, to receive that sweet kiss from you. The kiss that will rival all that ever kissed me before this.

Mmmmm . . . You wet me, as my wetness seeps through my panties, and our eyes slowly close from the magnetic strain of our lips becoming closer—then touch.

We feel it, the softness of our lips touching; wet, steamy, warm; then moist, as the tips of our tongues lightly explore one another's eagerly parted lips; softly at first, then trailing, tasting of us becoming one.

Gently, and careful, not wanting to rush the feeling, but wanting to let the passion of our kisses explode into a rage, but fighting the rage that builds within us.

Our kisses become stronger, deeper, more passionate, exciting, and intense. We both moan aloud as we release the passion that we make each other feel with the taste of our soft and sensual kisses.

You sit me on the countertop, gently, as if not to break me, kissing me, passionately, as I grab your face and kiss you deeper. Barely breathing, and taking deep breaths, we open our eyes to look into each other's and slowly pull away, not wanting to pull away, but wanting to see the affect that our kisses had on one another.

I lower my face from the embarrassment of that kiss, feeling that you could see all that I wanted; all that I desire from you and craved.

You smile a coy smile, touch my chin, and lift my face to yours with glistening eyes of fire to speak, "I want it too baby", you say with a soft and tender voice that caused me to shiver.

You then begin to fade away, as I turn onto my stomach, lifting one leg and cuddling the pillows on my bed; trying to fight becoming fully awake. I did not want the dream to end, but is it a dream? Is it that I was living this, and thinking about sleeping and dreaming this of you?

I begin to rock myself back into a deep sleep, hearing myself moaning, I feel my face smile, then I see you standing in front of me, right between my legs, while sitting on the countertop.

With my legs slightly parted, and my skirt lifted to where you can see the brightness of my panties, your hand cannot resist but to trail up my thigh and lightly touch them and my juices pour over your fingers as you touch me to a quaking orgasm, releasing months of pleasure, the pleasure of being untouched, now touched.

Mmmmm . . . You awaken me, making me want you, making me crave you into sleepless nights of tangled sheets, whispering deep voices and moaning; penetrating the silence of my warm body with sweats of pure lust.

WHEN THE NIGHT FALLS

As the light from the outside fades into darkness, blanketing my room with its warmth. The shadows of what I thought were you creeps into the corners of my eyes. I look—and they are just shadows.

It is funny how the thought of you just pops into my mind like that. Out of nowhere, just like that, and my focus is on nothing but you, no matter what else I do, I cannot shake you.

As I draw the curtains closed, I stop to stare at the steady darkening day turn into night. The moon crookedly rises into the sky, peaking from behind velvet clouds, as if it to whisper secrets of you down to me in a silent beauty that made my gaze linger.

Climbing into my warm . . . soft . . . bed, feeling the softness of the covers as I pull them up and over my naked body, I welcome the touch of them like a lover; like you, when I feel the touch of your strong hands touching my body.

When the night falls . . .

I think of you like this, I get lonely for you, for your touch, your kisses, and the heaviness of your body on top of mine, that pressure of your manliness sinking down onto me; to take my breath away; literally you take my breath away.

I sink into the center of my bed, closing my eyes to reveal a darker night behind them, and my mind forms a solid shadow of you that comes to me in softness, and in deep breaths. I touch my hands between my breasts and feel my heart begin to pound as the rise of my chest drops heavily with every trembling breath outward.

You make me—so wet.

So wet that my juices begin to flow steadily from my pussy, wetting my inner thighs, slowly creaming down between my ass, then to my sheets.

I feel my breath enter my lungs with intensity, expanding my chest as I scratch my belly and rib cage; grabbing hard my breasts into both my hands.

Hmmmm . . . When the night falls . . .

The crickets begin to chirp outside of my door rejoicing to the sounds, the moans, and the sighs of me pleasuring myself, thinking thoughts of you, calling your name in whispers of ecstasy; while my hand slides down the smoothness of my waist, allowing my fingers to guide me to my juicy wet pussy that swells with thoughts of you.

With the imaginary feel of you.

Pausing for a moment, I open my eyes, picturing your face on the ceiling above me, not wanting to cum just yet. Calming my breathing as I focus my thoughts on your face, on your eyes that glare of Caribbean waters, and white sand beaches.

I—taste you.

Yessss . . .

I can taste your saltiness on my lips, as I close my eyes breathing deep, kneeling down to lick your thickening shaft as if it were ice-cream; then to take it deep into my mouth, wrapping my tongue softly around it, squeezing it with the pressure of my full lips, feeling the girth of it thicken to where I can feel every vein that pumps with the uncontrolled throbbing and jerking of it.

Mmmmm . . . When the night falls . . .

My sheets are tangled and wet around my quivering body, and the moon peeks through the cracks of the curtains secretly watching as my body begins to shiver from the orgasm that builds with such urgency—I can barely contain it.

The chirping of the crickets begins fading into silence, as they listen to my intense breathing and I sink my fingers deep inside of myself.

I reach my hand to taste the wetness of my juices, and smelling the smell of myself on my fingertips drove me into deep strokes across my clit, while my cream oozes onto my fingers slipping and sliding from a slow soft rubbing motion—of wanting you inside of me.

My mouth slightly parts with quivering lips whispering your name into the night; my body begins to quake with the rage of my intense orgasm as I stroke myself frantically, grinding my hips into my fingers, squinting my eyes to see images of you behind them.

Then—I cum.

I cum screaming your name, cumming so hard that the moon shies away from my window in embarrassment, and there is total silence except for me screaming your name into the nights air, silencing all of nature's creatures outside my door, as my juices squirt onto my fingers and pond into the center of my sheets . . . leaving me completely drained—Wet!

I wither.

Breathing your name one last time.

Panting.

Moaning.

Feeling every part of my being pounding.

I feel and hear my heartbeat within my ears, drowning into your image, as I cum my last cum into a deep . . . peaceful . . . sleep.

When the night falls.

THE QUICKIE

Our juices began to flow, making that wet squishy sound.

Stirring up the earthy smells of our sweet lusty grinding that escapes from underneath the covers—filling the room.

Mmmmm . . .

Lips touching, hair pulling, moans of pleasure ringing in my ears as you flip me over to mount me from behind. Spreading my hips round and wide as you push to enter me.

Dropping to my elbows with a dip in my back, I moan from your strong hands gripping my ass, pulling it towards you, looking down at you spreading into me.

Sliding—into me.

"Aaawwwww shit baby!!" You growl, pushing yourself deep, licking your lips with eyes wide, listening to the sounds of air escaping my tight little pussy, as we fuse into each other's bodies; grinding into the rhythm of one.

You fill me up.

Sinking, spreading, pushing, gasping at the tight ring of cum forming around your shaft. Watching as you spread me to the point of splitting.

Cinda "Cin" Cianelli

I grab the covers as I bury my face deep to scream out in pain and pleasure, hiking my ass higher into the air as you stroke deep into my juiciness.

Flesh slapping, moaning words of pleasure, with the steamy lusty earthy smells becoming stronger, filling your nostrils, driving you into madness as you lean forward, pounding me so hard that I begin to slide off the foot of your bed.

I touch my hands to the floor, tangled amongst the covers, lifting my ass up higher, grinding harder into you.

You grip your footboard, slamming yourself deeper into me, biting my back—fucking me intensely.

Wait!!

Wait!!

I holler out as I begin to slide further off of your bed, bringing one leg to the floor, trying to balance both of us at the same time on my back, as you continue to thrust harder into me with no mercy.

I slowly slide onto the floor, entangled in your sheets; rolling over onto my back to see you standing above me stroking your thick-hard shaft. I lay their with my legs apart teasing you, teasing my swollen wet peach, grinding into my fingers and lifting my ass up from the scattered bedding on the floor.

You smile as you kneel down, coming face to face with my pussy, you inhale my scent deep while gripping your shaft tightly into your fist.

Lick

Lick

Your tongue strokes itself across my juiciness causing my clit to peak itself outside its door, wanting to be caressed by your warm mouth and tongue.

Lick

Lick again.

Then your warm moist mouth cups it as you begin to suck and pull it until it looks like the pit of a fresh ripe peach; causing me to grind into your mouth.

I cum so intensely, that I nearly smothered myself in the covers.

You come up licking my taste from your lips, to kiss me wet, soft, and juicy. Smearing the smells of me onto my lips, and the earthy smell intoxicates me into another orgasm.

You lift my legs up onto your shoulders, and push yourself slowly inside of me, then pull out to rub my swollen clit with the thick head of your shaft.

My back arches away from the floor, and I shift my hips to guide you deeper into my creaminess as I orgasm again.

I feel your throbbing warmness spreading me as I look into your face; your eyes are low as you make slow, short pumping motions, smiling a smile of intense lust, as my large round breasts begin to bounce to the rhythm of your push.

I run my fingers through my hair then pile the covers underneath my head to look down at you enter me.

Your strokes are long and deep.

I can see you in my belly as you move in and out of me. Leaning forward, you grab my breast pinching my thick nipple causing me to eke out in pleasure and mini orgasms.

"Are you ready baby", I am going to cum so hard." you say in a growling tone as your strokes intensify.

"Not yet baby, not yet", I say frantically, looking into your eyes as they turn boyishly in disagreement.

I smile lowering one leg from your shoulder to rest it onto the floor and lift my ass up to push against your thrust.

"Aaawwwww yeah baby, shit; keep doing that, just like that; I want to cum like this!!" You speak in almost a whisper.

You wrap both your arms around my leg that rests against your chest, and begin to slam deep into my wetness; grinding in perfect rhythm, I feel my wet pussy wrap tighter around your thickening shaft. I grab hold of your arms, trying not to claw through your skin as my orgasm draws nearer and my body begins to tremble.

"Do me just like that baby, yeah, just like that, harder, Harder, HARDER DAMMIT!!" I screamed out into your face!

"Keep talking like that baby, you are going to make me cum so hard!!" You say, as you reposition yourself to push all the way inside of me.

Your thrusts became so intense, you touch bottom almost shooting me across the room with such an intense orgasm that my upper body was half way underneath your bed.

You grab hold of the footboard still pumping harder and deeper into me. Right when you were ready to cum, you scream out, "Oh shit baby, I am going to cum, oh fuck yeah!!"

You pull out of me and yank me from underneath the bed, with one instant movement, gripping and jerking your shaft as you cum all over my bouncing breasts.

You stroke it intensely as I squeeze them together then slide your throbbing shaft right between them, cumming your last cum while holding onto the footboard of your bed.

Breathing heavily, we stare into each other's eyes; bodies jerking, trembling, struggling to catch our breath.

You fall over onto the floor, lying by my side; as we gasp ourselves into a deep, wet, sticky sleep—smiling.

WATCHING ME DRESS

You arrived at my loft, ringing the doorbell with anticipation. You are early for our date handsome, a night on the town filled with wine, dancing, and some serious public flirting with one another.

I have been waiting for this date for a long time.

The doorbell rings again as I wrap myself in a large fluffy white towel that reveals my smoothly waxed legs and freshly lotioned body.

The studio lights from the ceiling reflects from my brownish red skin, revealing its softness, and defines my lean toned body. I dim the lights to set the mood before I open the door.

"Hmmmm, you are early", I say aloud, and I know why, I know what you want baby—you want to watch me dress.

I remove the towel from my hair and shake out my freshly, vanilla-scented dreadlocks that fall over my face and shoulders. The music is already set for a sensual mood and turned down low; every candle in my place is burning, giving it a sultry look as the smell of vanilla fills the air.

The mosquito netting is hanging from the rafters, draping down and piled to the floor, surrounding my bed like a sheer wall; while the light from the candles bounce off the hardwood floors and set a lusty love scene.

I love my new place; it has such a sensual Caribbean feel and look to it, making me feel so sexy.

There is just one thing I need to do before I open the door; I grab my 6" luscious black pointed-toe heels, put them on and readjust the towel to where my breasts are slightly revealed and hurry to greet you.

As I open the door slowly, you have your back to me, in your black suit and overcoat, looking and smelling so damned good.

I see the flowers peeking over your shoulder as you turn around slowly, with that warm sexy smile that instantly turned to lust, seeing me standing there in a towel, with high heels on, and skin glistening in the dim lighting.

"Aaaaah, you brought me flowers and a gift?" I say as I kiss you on the lips, grabbing your hand, guiding you into my place—smiling.

I walk toward the cabinet, leaving you standing in the middle of the room, wondering what was in the beautifully wrapped gift box.

As I bend over to reach underneath the sink to pull out a vase, my towel lifts up just enough to reveal everything you wanted to see. Revealing more than you could handle at that moment.

Yes handsome—I knew that you where watching.

I put the flowers and water into the vase and placed it on the table, I walk slowly back across the room to the oversized loveseat where you sat, and sat down next to you; crossing my long legs, I could hear you sigh when they rested, leaning against yours.

I kiss you again on your lips as you hand me the small thin box. First removing the bow, I then open the packaging that was in my favorite shade of yellow, removing the tissue paper to reveal a pair of silk thigh-high stockings.

"Thank you baby!!" I say, kissing your lips with soft little kisses that aroused us both.

We stop and stare into each other's eyes as you whisper to me, "You are so beautiful." I stand up to go and finish getting ready, and as I did, the towel falls to the floor, revealing all of me, me, glistening in the dim lighting and flickering candles.

I stand there for a moment as your mouth dropped open, then bend over right in front of your face to pick the towel up from the floor.

Coming up slowly as your hand reaches out for my ass, and my smoothly waxed moist mound of juiciness, I glance back and stand there long enough for you to feel the firmness of my ass, and just as I feel your hot breath drawing near it all—I step away.

"We are going to be late!" I say as I take slow lingering strides across the floor, wrapping the towel around my shimmering body; then slip behind the mosquito netting walls of my bedroom, to get dressed.

The candles and dim lighting causes you to see the shape of my entire body as I remove the towel and my heels.

"Fix us a glass of wine baby, please?" I asked, while I slipped into my lacey black crotchless thongs with the garters attached.

Yes baby—Just for you.

You knew how much I love thigh-high stockings and the sexiness that they make me feel when I wear them. You knew that I would be aroused all night long from the way they rubbed against my freshly waxed long legs, along with the wine, and gazing into your handsome face all night baby.

I could see your face as I prepared to put the stockings on, while sitting on the edge of a beautifully padded chair next to my bed, behind the almost transparent netting, slowly teasing you, as if I did not know you were watching.

You intensely pour the wine into the second glass, almost overfilling it while your eyes enlarged as I stood up, placing my foot onto the edge of the chair and began pulling the stocking slowly up my long leg; making love to it as it caressed my smooth skin.

As I pull it up my thigh, and pull the garter strap down to connect it, I bend over slightly to where my ass became firmer, separating, and exposing the ribbons that held the crotchless thongs closed.

I can see you out of the corner of my eye, loosening your tie and gulping down the overfilled glass of wine like it was cold water on a hot desert night.

I smile to myself as I sit down, then slowly lie onto my back, lifting my bare leg into the air to put on the other stocking.

Slowly pulling it down, I clamp it onto the garter, sit up and slide my heels on, and out the corner of my eye you are standing there in the midst of the netting holding two glasses of wine, as you gaze upon my body like it is a sweet piece of chocolate.

"You are going braless tonight baby?" You ask, as your eyes become low with the most erotic look I have ever seen on your face, then I smile that coy smile of mischievousness.

Mmmmm, I got you baby, I got you right where I want you.

I step towards you, holding your hand with both of mine and tip the glass of wine to my lips, sipping it slowly while I look into your lusty eyes.

As I sip the wine from the glass, you kiss and nibble my fingers. I lift two of them to slowly slip them into your mouth, and you begin to suck and lick them, causing me to become so aroused, I begin to take big gulps of the wine myself, as we stand there, looking into each other's eyes—wanting each other badly.

I slowly pull my fingers from your soft wet mouth, and your eyes go low, with the want of more.

"We have to get going baby!" I say, knowing that, at this point, we are not going anywhere. I turn the fan on low, causing the candles to flicker wildly and the netting around my bed to sway in a slow, erotic rhythm, while the sensual music hum low in the background.

You refill our glasses of wine, as you continue to watch me dress.

You take off your jacket and lay it across the sofa, and stand there behind it, looking, watching, waiting; swaying to the music, and to the mosquito netting surrounding my bed, as if to be entranced.

I bend to reach for my dress off of the bed, and one of the garters across my ass pops loose, and dangles freely. I could see you flinch and your nipples harden through your shirt.

I smile slightly, and feel my panties instantly become moist, filling up with the creaminess of my lust for you, and you wanting to taste it, to taste me, to taste that smooth warm freshly waxed juiciness in your mouth; stirring it with your tongue and lips.

Mmmmm . . . My body shutters from the very thought of that visual.

I slide the little black dress down over my head and it falls freely, right below my ass.

Yes handsome—the backless one.

I put one foot on the chair, lift my dress up just enough to expose a tiny bit of my black lace thongs, and the lose garter lay there dangling from underneath. I look up from the task to see your eyes open wide, to be able to see all that is me underneath my dress, as you notice the little bows that tied my crotchless thongs closed, and the creamy white moistness that has started to seep through them.

You spill your wine down the front of your white dress shirt, and at this point, you show no concern, because you know that we are not going anywhere tonight handsome.

I lift my dress up a little more to connect the top of the stockings to the garter, putting one foot on the chair and slightly bending over, revealing to you the roundness of my full ass.

You sit there on the arm of the sofa, watching it all with an intense look of want, fully erect, and your mouth watering as I reach again to connect the back garter to the stocking.

"Baby!" I say, slowly turning around as the garter belt pops lose again, "Can you help me with this?"

You immediately finish off your glass of wine, grab mine from the table and walk to me quickly, trying not to spill it. You lift the glass to my lips, and as I drink from it, you kiss my cheek, then nibble at my neck.

I feel a gush of moistness push through my swollen mound, and the ribbons on my panties begin to strain.

I put one leg up on the chair, and feel the wetness starting to moisten my inner thigh. You slowly slide your hand between my legs, and I feel your body jerk when your fingers touch the wetness that you caused to ooze from my sweet peach.

"Oh shit baby, what are you trying to do to me?" You ask as you slowly lick my juices from your fingertips.

"I love the way you taste" You mumble, as I bend over to sit my glass of wine on the floor; not immediately realizing what I had done, and before I could stand, you drop to your knees and bury your face into my wet panties.

My body lunges forward as I hold onto the wall and mosquito netting, as my legs grow weak and quivering.

You use your lips and teeth to slowly untie one of the ribbons, and it pops lose with a snapping force.

Your body shakes as you put your hands on my ass to expose even more, as you moan and mumble words that I cannot understand.

I press my face against the wall, getting tangled in the mosquito netting and to brace myself as you press your face harder into the crevasse of my ass to untie the last bow that is straining to cage my swollen wet pussy.

It pops lose and your lips touch the smoothness of it all as you begin to explore my wetness with you tongue. You slap and grab my ass as you dive deeper into me with your tongue and face, causing me to scream aloud ripping into the netting to try and hold on, cumming so intensely that my body quakes, jerks and shutters with continuous orgasms. "Mmmmm baby", I say as the wine shoots through my body and to my head.

You lean back to look how swollen it has become, and when you do, I climb up onto the chair bending over with my ass spread wide so that you can see it all, you shake and dive into it again, licking it, tickling it, sucking it, causing it to swell even more as it gushes with my sweet cream.

"I can't take it anymore baby, please stop, wait, just one second, please baby, Ooooo shit please!!!!!!!!!" I cry out loud, trying to hold myself onto the chair.

I can hear you mumbling "Mmmmm Hmmmm baby, this is mine; you should have not teased me like that!" You repeat it over and over again, as my body weakened under the more than multiple orgasms you were giving to me.

Cinda "Cin" Cianelli

Almost to the point of passing out now, I reached behind me and grabbed you by the hair pulling you away from my juiciness, with the last bit of strength I had left.

I lift myself slowly, holding one hand on the wall, you stand and begin to remove your pants, I hold on trying to feel my legs and to get my balance, when I feel you grab me by the hips and probe for the opening with your throbbing thickness.

You grab my hair and pull it while biting on my shoulders and back, in doing that, my juices gush with a warmth that guided you to where you needed to be, and slide slowly into me, moaning something about how I teased you, and you are going to give me what I teased you for.

With my face pressed hard against the wall, I reach one hand around and grab your hair and you plunged a little deeper as you wrap one hand around my waist, pulling me into you hard, while the other hand held mine against the wall above my head, and there is no fighting back—no resistance.

You move your one hand down the center of my back, pushing me to bend over more, and I arch my back to where my ass is more exposed for you to see everything you are wanting to see. You grab me tighter around my waist with your arm and hand; the other hand slaps my ass, in such an electrifying way and sound, that I scream out with pleasure.

You slightly bend your knees preparing to enter me deeper as I feel you swell even more. I look back at you and you are looking down at it; watching it spread me wider and wider, tighter and tighter; your face so intense with the look of what you are seeing and feeling, just that alone caused me to ooze my wetness all over your thickness, and cause you to plunge even deeper.

You begin to growl like an animal now, reaching your hand around to feel my swollen peach and the juices that are dripping from it.

I gasp as you clasp it between your fingers and gently massage it to the rhythm of our bodies.

Your pace quickens as you tell me that you want to cum, my body shutters with the thought of how it will throb inside of me, causing my orgasms to multiply into hundreds of mini orgasms.

"Shit baby, I want to feel you, I want to feel it, I want to feel you cum now, cum inside me baby!!!!" I say in almost a scream, as I tightened around you, and you begin to buck like a madman, cursing, biting me, kissing me, telling me that you are going to cum.

Fucking cum in me baby, I want to feel it, I want to feel your hot cum! I want to feel you pulsating, give it to me, give it to me now dammit, as I grind harder against you, doing this thing with my ass that sends you into a mad rage.

You scream out, "Wait baby, don't do that, I do not want to cum yet, I do not want this to end just yet!!" You scream into the air, but it is too late, I have worked myself into a frenzy and getting ready to cum like I have never cum before.

"Ooh My God" I begin to scream as we have a perfect slamming rhythm going between us.

You pound me hard, and bury it into me harder, as I grip the covers, and begin to bite into the pillow. I work my ass against your thrust, taking it, taking it all as your body begins to quake.

"I'm cumming baby, I'm going to cum in your sweet chocolate pussy baby, I'm I'm Cummmmming FUCK!!!!!"

As I begin to feel the pulse of your shaft, I gush with sweet juices of my own, as we both begin to scream aloud, cursing, biting, feeling the feeling, feeling each other's touch, your thrust, my squeeze and it feels soooo damned good.

You continue to pound me harder, cumming, grabbing my ass, spreading it apart, watching it go in and out and all of my sweet cream wrapped in a messy circle around your shaft, and your juices plastered in my landing strip that has started dripping onto the chair.

With our legs weakening under the tremendous orgasms, you slowly pull me backwards towards my bed, and fall onto the mattress, almost hitting the floor, trying to keep it inside of me.

I cum again with my body shuttering, as you position us to lay on our side, hanging off the bed, with your pants still around your ankles, and my dress and thigh-high stockings badly stained with our juices.

We lie there sighing, shivering and breathing hard, "Wow" you say, as we begin to laugh. "I love to watch you dress baby." Where your last words before we fell asleep.

FINDING IN LOST

Finding in Lost . . .

"What does it mean to you?" You ask.

It means nothing, but everything, I think to myself.

Lying in my bed of darkened room, holding my phone tightly to my ear, wishing that you were lying right next to me and not asking such a riddle of a question.

Finding in lost.

Lost in finding.

My mind struggles with this thought.

I just want to be lost in your voice as the calmness of it soothes the finding of me, finding me lost in your arms of soft hair holding me to lose myself in your finding

I slide one foot off of my bed, touching the floor with tiptoe, letting my leg dangle, as if to ground myself to connect me to all that is real. As if to make the answer come to me instantly from feeling the coldness of my hardwood floor.

I search for the answer to your puzzle-like question that was such a simple one, but yet, it stirred in me a deep emotion that I could not put into words, as you silently await my answer.

Think, think, think, my brain starts to churn wondering if this was a test, a test to see if I was the one, and with no answer coming from me yet; I turn onto my side, placing a pillow in between my legs, and hold one in front of me as if it were you.

Think, think, think, my mind is saying to me, but not giving me an answer, as I fear you to become impatient—I stir.

Finding in lost, finding in lost, I repeat, while you continued to wait in silence.

While the words roll from my lips, I sink deeper into the emotion of your speak, trying to buy just a little more time while the clock tick ticks louder in my ear and the phone loses signal not regained.

I frustrate myself, turning onto my back with eyes staring into the darkness around me, hands in the cleavage of my breasts, feeling lost, feeling lost in you. I close my eyes and sink into your question . . . finding.

Finding in lost, finding in lost, my voice echoes softly.

Why can I not give an answer to such a simple question? My brain still wrestles me into thinking that I have lost in finding you, and you finding me; lost-out in finding my forever, my forever one.

I sink into the relaxed finding of the softness of my bed, closing my eyes; I am lost in the finding of your eyes that gaze into mine, your eyes that search into the finding of me lost inside of my clothes.

Finding the curves of my body with your hands as they become lost in the finding of my sensual parts that causes me to become lost in dizziness; lost in the arousal of your finding.

Finding, finding, echoes my mind.

Only the meaning comes to me separately, separating the words to give one definition at a time. Lost in this dizzying thing that causes me to slowly find the answer lost deep inside of me. Searching, but not yet finding the answer that you wish me to give, but lost in not knowing what your answer to this question is.

Dizzy, dizzy, dizzy, I become drunk with searching for the answer, lost in not knowing what the answer is to be, what it means to me.

Think, think, think.

Think of finding the answer, and not becoming lost in the finding of your lips so soft that they give me goose bumps to know that they will reach out and kiss mine soon.

Causing me to become lost in the softness of them, finding the tips of our tongues touching each other's, while lost in each other's finding.

Softly the kisses are, as I am lost in the thought of how it will be, lost in the wet gentleness of the way your soft juicy kisses will light a fire inside of me like a lighthouse.

Causing you to find me in the darkest of night from the bright hotness that will burn deep from within me; that you will light with the finding of your lips to mine.

I open my eyes to stare at the dark ceiling, trying to stay focused on what you think those words mean, thinking of what they mean to me. I slide back into myself thinking about how lost I was in finding the answer, but could not speak the answer, as the emotion of it drowned me deep into the finding—finding that I am lost for words.

It is all around me now!!
The Lost!!

Cinda "Cin" Cianelli

Clicking heels of my feet, hoping for them to take me to the answer of LOST IN FINDING!!!

I exhaust myself, as my body begins to wet with a soft glow of moisture and I slip into my mind of you finding me like this. Lying next to me with your hands trembling to touch, finding it hard for you to restrain touching the roundness of my breasts, and my nipples that stand in wanting to find your hands grip.

Finding myself lost in the feel of the roughness of them, lost for words, only to moan aloud in gasping breaths of finding the feeling to cause me to come alive with the finding of your touch.

Stay on the path, stay on the path to the question and answer my mind repeats to me; in a losing battle with my body becoming alive with finding the feeling that I know that you will give to me when we see each other in real.

Lost in the dreaminess that I find in your face, your eyes, your lips, your chest, your arms, your waist, your ass, your thick thighs and legs.

Lost!! Lost!! Lost!!

I am truly lost in you; not able to collect myself, my thoughts, the thoughts of your question, not even caring anymore in finding the answer . . . "LET THE FINDING STAY LOST!!" I scream in exhaustion!!

Contain myself, my mind grabs hold to bring me back to Finding In Lost!!

I quiver . . . as my sheets become wet with the sweats of being lost in the feel of you, the real of you, the finding in the hardening of your nipples that lie just beneath the tangle of soft dark hair of your muscular chest.

Lost!! Lost!! Lost!! Echoes my mind.

Finding that I am!

With no way out of this lost in finding. Sinking me deeper into the lost that I do not care to find any longer. The answer to your question is meaningless without you here with me!!

Lost in the craving of your hand sliding from my breast, as the pinch of your fingertips to my nipple lingers; losing me in the lost of moaning in your pleasure.

Finding me spreading my legs to you, with the feeling of your hands stirring into the swollen wetness of my pussy.

Lost in the feeling that quakes my body and yours, with stiff-like movements, finding it hard to hold back the orgasms that approach like a rage of lost finding.

Lost in our eyes meeting with the lustiness of finding in what we had lost so long ago, never to regain until now. Finding it in each other as our lips quiver to touch with warming, wet, kisses.

Hands touching body parts to come alive to no longer be lost, but finding all that we had lost outside of each other now inside.

My wetness drips from the tips of your fingers as you reach them to your open mouth and with tongue eager to taste, your eyes close with the finding of my creaminess, and you become lost in the taste of me.

Gently I grab your shaft squeezing it until you jerk with finding pleasures of my strong hands that grip you into lowering eyes, lost breath, and finding that you feel me deeper than you ever felt with anyone else before this moment.

Your juices peek from the head of your head in finding that there is nothing lost about what I am preparing you to find in me.

I lay you to your back as I straddle you. You grip your shaft into your hand to find the opening of my pussy, and I sink down slow onto you, no longer pondering the question of finding in lost, and you become lost in me, and I in you—finding.

Fucking you till the question is no longer a question in your mind, grinding you deep into me as you become lost in my pleasure that I am finding in you.

I look down at you, into your face, seeing that you are finding what I am feeling, lost deep into the pleasures of my pussy, tightly wrapped around your shaft to choke it into not searching for your finding in lost now!!

Working into a frenzy, I lift to put my hands onto your chest as you grab hold of my ass and I grind into you, feeling your hairy arms sensually rub against my skin—lost.

Lost into the sounds of each other's finding. Feeling the feeling of the finding of our intense orgasm that come to us out of shouting words, and moans of pleasure, no longer lost we scream from the inside as we buck and grind.

Finding!! Finding!! Grinding!! Grinding!!

Grinding deep onto you and you into me; feeling lost in the strong orgasm that we cause each other to find with our bodies clashing in heat and sweat!

With our sweat dripping into each other's sweat, with our eyes locked to each other's eyes, knowing that at this moment!!

With our intense orgasms exploding into a rage of fury within us, and outside of us; we have just sought the lost in finding!!

The finding in lost of us becoming one!!

COMING SOON!!!

Part Two

The Cindarotica Collection "I Am Cin"

- *More intense short stories*
- *More photos*
- *More of what you cum to me for*

"Cindarotica . . . When Sin Is Just Not Enough!"

Cinfully Cin
The Intensity Has Only Just Begun!!

THE ART OF THE BLOW

In candle light—

I watch the slow rise of it thicken with bulging veins, pumping iron-strength blood.

Swelling it into tightness, into heaviness, into a stiffness that causes my knees to weaken; sliding down the front of your body, clutching your thick thighs, looking upward, sneaking moments of your eyes open wide, looking intensely into mine.

Lips plump and wet, licking with tongue, tasting the sweetness of my mouth waiting to taste you.

I feel you shiver, and the moans that come from you echo so sensually, filling my ears with your deep voice that creams my pussy to swell and pulsate with desire.

Letting go, I stand and kiss your lips softly drinking you in. Tasting your lust in waves of pleasure, with the clashing of our tongues.

I like when you are like this, allowing me to take my time, and you struggle to hold back, so that you can feel the softness of what I want to give to you, and the way that I want to give it to you.

Slowly guiding you to the sofa, I motion for you to sit as I pull your pants down to your ankles and off with your shoes; flinging them across the room, making you realize that nothing else matters but this moment.

Cinda "Cin" Cianelli

I slide down between your legs with your hand in my hair, almost as if you are guiding me, but I am guiding myself, because tonight; I am craving you!! I am craving it!! Craving to taste your smoothness in my mouth and on my lips.

I whisper softly for you to let me taste it, while looking up to your face with big lusting eyes, then I . . .

TO BE CONTINUED . . . In book two of, "I Am Cin"

(Smile)

What is next for Cin and Cindarotica

The release of the second book from the Ten-Series Cindarotica Collection, called: "I Am Cin!!" Will be released during the late summer, or early fall of 2012. Other books from the collection will follow.

"I Am Cin", will be released with steamy-hot professionally taken, color photos of her in compromising positions, 90% nudity, but tastefully and Cinfully done.

Her book touring/signings will start mid to late summer of 2012 on the west coast of the United States. Keep a watch out for the maps, dates, and states that she will be touring in by viewing her links or Google her at: Cindarotica to keep up with what is going on in her Cinful world.

You can also tickle her Twitter at: Cindarotica, to keep up with her latest posts.

If you purchase a book during her book signing, she will gladly autograph it, and take a personal photo with you. So bring your camera, our use her photographer that will be onsite, for the best photo quality and exposure, and get that photograph autographed as well. (Smile)

Her Cinful Blog Page, on her website, Cindarotica.com will be up and running soon.

Winter of 2012, Cin will be releasing her dating book. This is an amazing book filled with **true stories**, thoughts, experiences, poetry, and love letters. The stories range from funny, loving, sad, scary, heartfelt, to WTF experiences.

The craziness that we all go through when it comes to dating, or searching for a mate; including the "What Ifs", logical thoughts, what is considered to be crazy approaches, or crazy things said; are all included in this wonderfully put together book. It is a fun and informative book to read. It will also come in audio book format, read by Cin herself.

If you are searching for her, and cannot find her anywhere, you can track her through Google, under: Cindarotica, but as an up and coming erotic writer, she will be all over the place, and will not be hard to find. (Smile)

Cin will be teaming up with one of her favorite alcohol beverage companies. Keep and eye out for that one!! All we can say is, "Dirty Girl Vodka Martini Please?!!

Thank you for purchasing this book, and be sure to purchase your super steamy, upcoming audio book version with sensual sound effects infused into her live reading, and yes, it is her voice. You will be truly entranced by her stories, and her very very sensual voice.

Thank you, and see you soon.

Links, Blogs, and more Cinful Information

Google Me: Cindarotica

www.Cindarotica.com

www.Twitter.com/Cindarotica

www.Youtube.com/Cindarotica

www.Meetup.com/CinfullyCin

www.Facebook.com/Cindarotica

www.Tagged.com/Cindarotica

www.BlackPlanet.com/CinfullyCin

www.Plentyoffish.com/CinfullyCin

www.MyYearbook.com/Cindarotica

www.OkayCupid.com/CinfullyCin

www.Badoo.com/CinfullyCin

www.Myspace.com/Cindarotica

www.WAYN.com/CinfullyCin

AUTHOR BIOGRAPHY

Cin was born in Cleveland, Ohio, where she spent the majority of her childhood, then moved with her parents and siblings to Overbrook, Oklahoma at the age of 15, then later moved to Ardmore, Oklahoma; where she spent close to four years, before moving back to Ohio, and has been residing in Las Vegas, Nevada over the past 18-years.

As a child, she showed an array of skills that caught the attention of all adults who encountered her. You could not help but to stop and stare at her with big eyes, and a gapping mouth, as she sung opera as a Soprano 1, better than a trained professional, at the age of seven years old (Damn!! She was born with that skill).

The following year, she started designing and sewing gowns as well as dresses, never using a sewing pattern. Later in years, creating her own line of gowns and mini dresses, in Cleveland, Ohio. She began to sale them to family, friends, and all others that wanted something sensually unique; she ultimately named her clothing line "The Haynesworth Dress". (Another skill that she was born with)

At the age of nine, she took a liking to reading; reading so much that sometimes she would read two books in one day. You ask her who her favorite author is, and without hesitation, she will say Shakespeare, and at the age of nine, she was also able to understand a vast amount of Shakespeare's work, and her favorite piece, she eagerly expresses, is Julius Cesar. She says in a hip-hop dialect, rolling her tongue ring across her lips with a crooked-lip smile; then stop to laugh at her silliness.

Also at that age she read books from fiction, romance, how to be a detective, the arts of sex, mechanics, travel, home renovation, logical thinking, books on self improvement, ballet, self defense, and business; teaching herself from every book that was in her grasp.

She is definitely a different type of woman, and sometimes I can see why she is still single, because it is going to take a very confident man to be with this chocolatey, soul-soothing, tall beauty that can send a man's loins into chaos with just words and her sensual voice; so imagine what it would be like to actually be with her.

Wheeeew Man Oh Man!!

Cin has been writing since 3rd grade, mainly poetry; then entering the age of 17, she began writing short love stories and poetry, most of her work, from her childhood, she keeps boxed up and stored away.

She began writing erotica seriously and steadily at the end of 2007, where her first piece was called "Taste", and from there, erotic stories and poetry continued to spill out from her pen.

She says that everything influences her writing, mainly a random word or sentence. She also states that being beyond super sensitive from the second grade until now, and with it growing more intense each year may have a lot to do with what and how she writes.

I laugh to myself when I once overheard her in a restaurant say that she could actually feel the taste of her food and can have orgasms from it.

Then went into explaining that this is what the food in Europe does to her, as well as sushi; while she sat there eating Salmon with a pair of red-tipped black porcelain chopsticks to her lips, rubbing her hand up and down her thigh while her toes began to curl in her 6" black, strappy, red-bottom toeless heels.

To know her personally, is to honestly and truly love her. She is very kind-hearted, always smiling and behind that smile is a very confident, goal oriented, giggly, but also a bit shy, and delightful female, that houses a vast amount of skills and knowledge in that sexy brain of hers.

She is truly very sensual, steamy, hot and lusty, but the crazy thing is; is that she does not know that she is, and that also makes her even more sexy, lovable, and wanted.

Her voice, as she reads her work or when she speaks, oozes erotica, and so does her eyes; they will drown you into wanting her.

She is a very happy-go-lucky woman with a warmth about her that penetrates you into smiles and her aura glows as she walks toward you smiling, she is truly a gem.

When she walks into a room, it is crazy how people stop and stare, then whisper, and admire this tall drink, as her body sways with grace in her 6 or 7" high heels; still owning the walk of a runway model, a title that she held for six years.

Yes, her work will definitely have you melting into a puddle of her. Hypnotizing you to be that man in her stories, while feeling her every word, making you feel her in ways that you have never felt a woman, and that is—without being physically touched!!

Hahaha!!! Damn, she is good, and I am not afraid to admit it!!

Getting to know Cin, some people say that she is very secretive, a very private person when she is not in the public's eye. I would not say secretive, as she has experienced more in her life than most, and do not mind sharing. It is just that she has experienced so much, there is much to tell, so she tells only small snippets, unless a person ask for more details.

Living alone as a single woman, writing, sometimes performing at open mics, dancing salsa all night long, country line dancing, or just going over to a friend's house for dinner, she is still a bit of a loner, spending a great deal of her time locked away—writing.

She explains that most people think that she is a party animal, with a long line of suitors that wrap around a couple of big-city blocks. Cin laughs aloud and says that she has never seen them, and she does not see them even now.

However, she deeply expresses that she wants only one, and supposes that she will know him when he is ready to come to her, as she is ready, but she states with confidence that she does not plan to settle, (with a big bright smile on her face).

Cin is truly a simple but complex woman, there are so many ways to describe her, but to shorten it, and explain her to a perfect stranger, well in the words that, we, her close friends describe her would be this:

Fun, funny, full of energy, positive, witty, tall, curvy, statuesque, chocolatey, educated, beautiful, sexy, sensual, steamy, giggly, always smiling, addictive, giving, creative, positive, loving, adventuress, loner, kind, confident, somewhat fearless, not afraid to speak her mind (with kindness), have a plethora of skills and knowledge, and the most down-to-earth person that you will probably ever meet.

And she thinks that she is just a girl in a woman's body. She is more, she is truly an amazing person, and we are glad to call her friend.

We Love You Cin!!

-Your Friends-